The Silence of the Sea
Le Silence de la mer

The Silence of the Sea
Le Silence de la mer

*A Novel of French Resistance
during World War II by "Vercors"*

Edited by James W. Brown and
Lawrence D. Stokes

Oxford • New York

First published in 1991 by **Berg**

Editorial offices: 150 Cowley Road, Oxford OX4 1JJ, UK
838 Broadway, Third Floor, New York, NY 10003-4812, USA

Berg is an imprint of Oxford International Publishers Ltd.

Paperback Edition 1993
Paperback edition reprinted in 1996, 1999, 2002, 2003

Library of Congress Cataloging-in-Publication Data
Vercors, 1902–
  [Silence de la mer. English]
  The silence of the sea : a novel of French resistance during World
War II = Le silence de la mer / by Vercors : edited by James W. Brown
and Lawrence D. Stokes
     p. cm.
  Translation of: Le silence de la mer.
  Includes bibliographical references.
  ISBN 0–85496–671–4
  ISBN 0–85496–378–2 (pbk)
  1. World War, 1939–1945—Underground movements—France—
Fiction.
I. Brown,, James w., 1934–.   II. Stokes, Lawrence D.III. Title.
IV. Title: Silence de la mer.
PQ2603.R924S513   1991
843´.914—dc20   90–39336
                                                                                                            CIP

British Library Cataloguing in Publication Data
The silence of the sea / Le silence de la mer:
A novel of the French resistance during World War II by "Vercors".
  I. Brown, James W.   II. Stokes, Lawrence D.
  843.912[F]

  ISBN 0–85496–671–4
  ISBN 0–85496–378–2 (pbk)

Printed in the United Kingdom

Contents

Preface and Acknowledgments

Since its clandestine publication in German-occupied Paris during 1942, the novel *Le Silence de la mer* by the then little-known satirist Jean Bruller[†] (writing under the pseudonym of Vercors) impressed contemporaries around the world with the nobility of its message and the sensitivity of its language. Thus, a future head of government of the Canadian province of Québec recalled reading as a war correspondent stationed in London "that extraordinarily pure story . . . in which Vercors managed to create an oasis of beauty in the midst of barbarity." The editors of *Life* magazine, where a slightly abridged translation appeared in 1943, described it as "not only a distinguished piece of fiction, but also a brilliant piece of reporting on French resistance to the German occupation" and "perhaps the most remarkable literary product of this war."[1] To be sure, there were prominent anti-fascists who wrongly interpreted the book as a mere invitation to *attentisme* (wait and see) or, at best, passive opposition to Hitler's rule and therefore concluded that it was quite unrealistic by that stage in the conflict.[2] Jean Paulhan, France's leading editor and an associate of Vercors in the intellectual Resistance, jibed at his characterization of the young woman in the tale who could fall in love with the aristocratic occupier under her

1. Rene Lévesque, *Memoirs* (Toronto, 1986), p. 89; and *Life* 15 (11 October 1943): 103.

2. David Caute, *The Fellow-Travellers: A Postscript to the Enlightenment* (London, 1973), p. 199; and Jean-Pierre Azéma, *From Munich to the Liberation, 1938–1944* (Cambridge, 1984), p. 255; also A.J. Liebling, ed., *The Republic of Silence* (New York, 1947), pp. 174–75; Margaret Atack, *Literature and the French Resistance: Cultural Politics and Narrative Forms, 1940–1950* (Manchester, 1989), pp. 63–64; and Jean-Paul Sartre, *What is Literature?* (London, 1950), pp. 52–54. The discrepancy in contemporary reactions to the novel largely stemmed from the long delay between its completion (October 1941) and its actual appearance (late summer of 1942). See S. Beynon John, "The Ambiguous Invader: Images of the German in Some French Fiction about the Occupation of 1940–44," *Journal of European Studies* 16 (1986): 195–96; and Historical Introduction, below.

roof "without ever saying so much as 'good morning' to him." Arthur Koestler also found the story "psychologically . . . phoney" and, what was worse, politically "exasperating" in its negative attitude toward Germans hostile to Nazism; hence it resembled French behavior in interning exiles from Germany in 1939. Soviet author Ilya Ehrenburg, "writing from his devastated homeland where the Nazis razed villages and murdered their inhabitants," could not believe either in the "affable, persuasive" German officer depicted by Vercors or in a Resistance "sans knives and hand-grenades." Thereupon a London-based newspaper of General de Gaulle's Free French forces, *La Marseillaise*, performed a volte-face and denounced the author of the novel it had previously printed in its own pages as a "provocateur." Yet on the continent the Communist-controlled underground literary periodical *Les Lettres françaises* called the book "the most moving, the most deeply human that we have had the opportunity to read since the beginning of the German occupation."[3] This has been the judgment, too, of most subsequent writers on the "black years" of wartime France. In revealing to his disoriented countrymen the brutal aims of Nazi policies behind the still largely "correct" deportment of many benevolent Germans, Vercors's "justly celebrated" story not only "brilliantly served the necessities of Resistance propaganda" but also "registered a reality which historians have since endorsed in full," and is therefore in itself "as much a document as a novel."[4]

Although it was translated both in Britain (under the title *Put Out the Light*) and America as well as into numerous other languages, and several French editions appeared before and after 1945,[5] the book and its background are not always accurately remembered

3. Atack, *Literature and the French Resistance*, pp. 24, 41; Liebling, ed., *Republic of Silence*, p. 183; Arthur Koestler, *The Yogi and the Commissar* (London, 1945), pp. 26–27; Vercors, *The Battle of Silence* (New York, 1968), p. 255; and Herbert Lottman, *The Left Bank: Writers, Artists, and Politics from the Popular Front to the Cold War* (Boston, 1982), p. 184.

4. H.R. Kedward, *Occupied France: Collaboration and Resistance, 1940–1944* (Oxford, 1985), p. 11; James D. Wilkinson, *The Intellectual Resistance in Europe* (Cambridge, Mass., 1981), p. 38; and John F. Sweets, *The Politics of Resistance in France, 1940–1944: A History of the Mouvements unis de la Résistance* (DeKalb, Ill., 1976), pp. 20–21; but see also John, "The Ambiguous Invader," p. 196; and Stanley Hoffmann, *Decline or Renewal? France since the 1930's* (New York, 1974), p. 28: "The national situation of France . . . in the three-fifths of France occupied by the Germans . . . made it impossible for the French to practice *le silence de la mer*."

5. Vercors, *Battle of Silence*, p. 230; and L. Metzger, ed., *Contemporary Authors*, vol. 12 (Detroit, 1984), p. 93.

even by authors who recognize its significance as "the most famous 'Resistance' novel written at the time." Frequently confused is the relationship between the two French figures, an elderly man and his young niece. Some writers transpose her into his daughter, others make him a woman, or both. And in one account, more than a single person is imagined to have been concealed under the nom de plume of Vercors.[6]

The purpose of the present bilingual edition, the first such in French and English, is to introduce Vercors's tale to a generation without personal experience of World War II, who may or may not be able to read it in its original tongue. By placing the novel within the historical context of the awakening Resistance in France to the devastating implications of Nazi rule, especially as this affected French literary life and the role played by intellectuals in general during the Occupation, the editors hope to enhance appreciation of this unique book and of the other publications that followed from the secret "Editions de Minuit" (Midnight Press) launched by Vercors with *Le Silence de la mer*. The concept of "silence" chosen by the author to exemplify his rejection of collaboration with his country's temporary masters is also discussed in its ramifications for literature and philosophy. Readers will be further aided in understanding the texts by the annotation provided for the English version together with an extensive glossary of French terms. Finally, for those who wish to pursue study of either the Resistance or Vercors's subsequent career as one of France's foremost postwar writers, an annotated list of relevant books and articles is appended.

The editors would like to acknowledge first and foremost the active encouragement of Jean Bruller in the preparation of this edition of his novel. He not only consented to an interview early in 1988 at his Paris home, but also greatly assisted in resolving the difficult matter of the publication rights to the book. We are grateful to the firm of Editions Albin Michel whose 1964 "édition définitive" of *Le Silence de la mer* is here reprinted, as well as to Ms. Danielle Coleman of Macmillan London Limited for permission to use Cyril Connolly's

6. Robert O. Paxton, *Vichy France: Old Guard and New Order, 1940–1944* (New York, 1972), p. 38; J.H. King, "Language and Silence: Some Aspects of French Writing and the French Resistance," *European Studies Review* 2 (1972): 229; Alexander Werth, *France, 1940–1955* (New York, 1956), p. 169; and Jørgen Haestrup, *European Resistance Movements, 1939–1945: A Complete History* (Westport, Conn., 1981), p. 65.

excellent translation, which was first published in 1944. Dr. Lise-lotte Jünger clarified an important question concerning Ernst Jünger's inspiration for the novel. A number of colleagues helpfully provided various forms of scholarly advice: Professors John C. Cairns, Christopher English, John F. Godfrey, Jack Kolbert, Michael R. Marrus, Robert O. Paxton, the late Henri Peyre, John F. Sweets, and members of the Dalhousie History Department seminar. At different stages the manuscript was expertly word processed by Mary Wyman and Kathrin A. Stokes; funding for this work was provided by the Dalhousie University Research Development Fund for the Humanities and Social Sciences. Finally, Vercors's own fascinating account of his wartime experiences, *The Battle of Silence*,[7] constitutes an invaluable source on the immediate background to the novel and has therefore been drawn upon extensively, though not uncritically, in our introductions.

James W. Brown   Halifax, Canada
Lawrence D. Stokes

---

7. Translated by Rita Barisse from *La Bataille du silence* (Paris, 1967); see Naomi Bliven, "Keeping a Secret," *The New Yorker* (8 November 1969): 203.

Historical Introduction
Lawrence D. Stokes

In November 1941, with almost all of Europe firmly under Nazi control and Hitler's armies inside the suburbs of Moscow, Jean Bruller, a graphic artist and before the war the author of several volumes of satirical drawings, sought out his Parisian printer Ernest Aulard with an unexpected request.[1] Although clandestinely published newspapers, beginning with the anonymously edited *Pantagruel* in October 1940, and even periodicals such as the Communist *La Pensée libre* for which Bruller had agreed to write had already been in circulation,[2] his proposal was more ambitious. It was for the establishment of an underground publishing house that would produce books of a length and quality beyond the capacity of any fugitive journal and yet designed as carefully as in peacetime. Besides providing an outlet first of all for a manuscript Bruller had completed (it was *Le Silence de la mer*) but which the Gestapo's recent seizure of *La Pensée libre* prevented appearing, the planned enterprise would give other authors unwilling to publish subject to German censorship the opportunity at last to see their work unsullied in print. What was more, such a series of volumes with the "current of thought" they would inevitably reflect would furnish proof abroad "that French intellectual life survived under the Nazi heel. . . . France, amid misfortune and violence, was able to keep faith with her highest purpose: her claim to think straight." Broadsheets and propaganda tracts that overtly aimed to arouse popular resistance to the occupying power were not suited to fulfill this task; only books could. Bruller was encouraged by his longtime friend, Pierre de Lescure, a novelist and bookseller earlier enrolled

1. See Vercors, *Battle of Silence*, pp. 159–61; also Jacques Debû-Bridel, *Les Editions de Minuit: Historique et bibliographie* (Paris, 1945), pp. 21–29.
2. Henri Noguères and others, *Histoire de la Résistance en France de 1940 à 1945*, vol. 1, *La première année, Juin 1940–Juin 1941* (Paris, 1967), pp. 163–64, 310, 422, and illustration following p. 384; Azéma, *From Munich to the Liberation*, p. 79; Debû-Bridel, *Les Editions de Minuit*, pp. 17–21; and Vercors, *Battle of Silence*, pp. 128–30, 134–37, 153–54.

in a (meanwhile defunct) network of the British intelligence service that had gathered information and organized escape routes for agents and airmen,[3] who agreed to take on responsibility for uncovering the authors of further suitable texts. Not without some trepidation, for many small businessmen had become pro-German, Bruller arrived to sound out "le petit père Aulard." After carefully reconnoitering each other's current political attitudes, the considerably older tradesman of working-class origin and the bourgeois intellectual found to their mutual pleasure that they were of the same mind "on the Red Army's resistance, on Britain's tenacity," and similar subjects. Unfortunately, however, Aulard had to admit that his firm employed too many people to guarantee the indispensable degree of security for the project Bruller had in mind. But he did undertake to find a smaller printing shop where the job stood a better chance of being carried out safely. His choice fell on that of Georges Oudeville, who worked alone, turning out wedding and funeral cards, in premises across from a German military hospital. With a single press and enough fine type provided by Aulard to set up a folio of eight pages at a time, Oudeville would require three months in between his regular employment to complete by hand the 96-page volume Bruller foresaw. And "who would imagine anybody crazy enough to print subversive material under the enemy's very nose?"[4]

The willing participation of Aulard – who also donated the paper on which the initial edition of *Le Silence de la mer* was printed – and Oudeville in the undertaking was not alone sufficient to hold out the promise of success. There remained, for instance, the need to secure adequate financial support to cover other costs. This was forthcoming through the mediation of Bruller's own banker, for the most part from the personal account of the latter's employer. A difficult technical problem was sewing and binding the pages together when the printer had finished his task. Another friend of Bruller since childhood, Yvonne Paraf, agreed to turn her apartment into the de facto business office of the new enterprise, where

3. Ibid., pp. 90, 102, 108, 116–18, 153–55. Vercors, who had contributed to a literary periodical put out by Lescure, also joined him in this underground activity.
4. On the crucial importance of especially small-scale printers for the success of the Resistance, which initially – and to a considerable degree throughout the Occupation – involved the production of newspapers and other published material that cost many of them their lives, see Azéma, *From Munich to the Liberation*, pp. 157, 255; and Kedward, *Occupied France*, p. 52.

she and a handful of female volunteers recruited by her folded, collated, and stitched the books that were then hidden in closets and cupboards to await distribution. This proved perhaps the most daunting part of the entire operation. Its eventual resolution, which encompassed both the delivery of copies to selected individuals in the Paris area and of bulk quantities to loyal helpers elsewhere around the country, took many months – and much daring – to arrange satisfactorily.[5] Finally, the actual identities of all those involved understandably had to be concealed. In his role as a writer, Bruller chose – among other aliases – that of Vercors after the imposing massif near Grenoble where he had been demobilized at the conclusion of the fateful campaign of 1940. (Four years later this ironically became the site of a disastrous operation by the *maquis*, as the armed partisan Resistance groups in southern and eastern France were known, against German forces and their French auxiliaries.)[6] Neither his wife nor his mother could be informed who Vercors really was or for that matter be allowed to read what he wrote lest they recognize places and persons described in it. Even before *Le Silence de la mer* was formally published, while it was circulating in manuscript form among a few trusted readers, speculation about the author's identity was rife. It was only fully revealed after 1945, which led the poet Louis Aragon to comment wryly that this was "the one true secret of the war." As a publisher in his dealings with Oudeville and others, Bruller was called Drieu, a "malicious" choice since it was the name of the collaborationist intellectual Pierre Drieu la Rochelle, who in 1940 had taken over the editorship of France's most prestigious literary periodical, the *Nouvelle Revue Française*. Yvonne Paraf, ignorant about the man behind the pseudonym Vercors with whom she met almost every day, adopted the nom de guerre of Desvignes, and Vercors appeared as Monsieur Desvignes in contacts they made together.[7]

5. Vercors, *Battle of Silence*, pp. 43, 162–64, 172, 178–80, 188–89, 196, 202–4.
6. This dramatic incident touched Vercors personally; see ibid., pp. 270–71 and his homage "Jean Prévost le fort" to the friend and literary critic shot while commanding the *maquis* in the battle, reprinted in Vercors, *Portrait d'une amitié et d'autres morts mémorables* (Paris, 1954), pp. 99–108.
7. Vercors, *Battle of Silence*, pp. 47, 82–83, 165–67, 172–73, 181–82, 224–25, 229, 233–35, 243, 245, 265, 279; and Debû-Bridel, *Les Editions de Minuit*, pp. 29–31, 47–48. Even the latter history of the publishing enterprise, which appeared at the end of the war, concealed Bruller's full name on the grounds that he was pursuing another career and did not wish to profit improperly from Vercors's fame. See ibid., p. 18.

In this fashion was born the Editions de Minuit, which in several respects was a creation typical especially of the early phase of the French Resistance. For one thing, this initial period utilized the printed word more frequently than the gun or the bomb in opposing Nazi hegemony, though in the case of the Editions it took the unusual form of books rather than leaflets or a newspaper. Indeed, most of what eventually became the principal such organizations within France – e.g., Combat, Franc-Tireur, Libération – either began or were closely identified with a paper of the same name; and if not *L'Humanité*, the official organ of the French Communist Party (PCF), then other publications associated with it preceded the bulk of PCF activists in moving to resist the Nazis.[8] Then, too, this usually began among a handful of persons, as a rule close friends and acquaintances enjoying mutual confidence and a shared outlook about the nature of France's situation in the wake of the shocking defeat at the hands of Germany and the need to take steps – of whatever sort – to counteract its effects.[9] But what led a particular individual to reach a decision to embark upon deeds fraught with acute personal danger? Though there is no universally valid formula as to the elements constituting the mentality of those among the French who became resisters (any more than there was a shared social background among them), by tracing the biography of Vercors we can glimpse why at least one man chose that path.

Jean Marcel Adolphe Bruller was born in Paris on 26 February 1902. His mother was of Catholic origin and his father, a publisher, Jewish.[10] Louis Bruller, to whose memory and probable fate at the hands of the Nazis – had he not died before the war – Vercors devoted the second of his longer publications in the Editions de Minuit,[11] deeply cherished France (to where he had walked as a

8. Sweets, *Politics of Resistance*, pp. 14, 43; and King, "Language and Silence," p. 231. There is a balanced analysis of the still disputed issue of French Communist attitudes toward the German occupier prior to Hitler's invasion of the Soviet Union on 22 June 1941 in Azéma, *From Munich to the Liberation*, pp. 81–85.

9. See Sweets, *Politics of Resistance*, p. 33; and Peter Novick, *The Resistance versus Vichy: The Purge of Collaborators in Liberated France* (London, 1968), p. 15.

10. Vercors, *Battle of Silence*, pp. 140, 166, 192; and R.D. Konstantinović, *Vercors écrivain et dessinateur* (Paris, 1969), p. 10.

11. This was *La Marche à l'étoile*, which first appeared in December 1943; a translation was published as *The Guiding Star* (London and New York, 1946). Vercors, *Battle of Silence*, pp. 221, 243–46; Atack, *Literature and the French Resistance*, pp. 88–90; and Pierre Brodin, *Présences contemporaines* (Paris, 1956), vol. 1, *Littérature*, pp. 325–27. All but some 12,500 of the over 75,000 Jews living in France whom the Nazis murdered (the great majority of them either foreigners or, like

youth from his native Hungary) as the home of liberty and justice. To his son he thus bequeathed not only a republican patriotism, but also the association with a minority that was almost automatically excluded after 1940 from collaboration with the Germans.[12] Following graduation from the Ecole Alsacienne in the capital and a period of military service in North Africa, young Bruller studied electrical engineering at the University of Paris and a technical college and received his diploma in 1922. He had already decided, however, not to make use of this training but instead to pursue a career as an artist and engraver. This was solidly launched four years later with the appearance of his first album of satirical drawings on "21 Delightful Ways of Committing Suicide" (as it was called in the 1930 translation), which was inspired by his relationship with Yvonne Paraf and which was a considerable popular and artistic success. Prior to the outbreak of World War II he published several more volumes of drawings as well as providing illustrations or introductions for a number of other works, including Rudyard Kipling's "Puck of Pooks Hill" and editions of Racine, Coleridge and Poe. In light of both his developing political beliefs and subsequent literary accomplishment under the Nazi Occupation, two of these early productions are particularly worth noting: one was a collection of watercolors, *Visions intimes et rassurantes de la guerre* (1936), the other was simply entitled *Silences* (1937). The former, which depicted a variety of people with a rosy view of a future war from which they hoped to profit,[13] pointed to what was Bruller's chief conviction in relation to interwar French and European politics: his pacifism.

As a schoolboy during the First World War, he had initially relished the conflict and hated the Germans "with serenity." Before its end, however, an embittered officer on leave from the fighting had disillusioned Bruller so thoroughly that henceforth he came to

---

Vercors's father, naturalized French citizens) had been deported to the east with the cooperation of Vichy governmental and police authorities by the end of 1943. See Michael R. Marrus and Robert O. Paxton, *Vichy France and the Jews* (New York, 1981), pp. 343, 372.

12. See Richard Cobb, *French and Germans, Germans and French: A Personal Interpretation of France under Two Occupations, 1914–1918/1940–1944* (Hanover, New Hampshire, 1983), pp. 73–74; but also Vercors, *Battle of Silence*, pp. 175–76 for at least one example of Jewish collaboration with Vichy anti-Semitism.

13. Vercors, *Battle of Silence*, pp. 15–16, 102–4; Konstantinović, *Vercors*, pp. 10–11, 28–29, 187–92; and Brodin, *Présences contemporaines* 1:323.

regard modern warfare as a profound abomination on account of its unspeakable suffering and senseless killing. Thanks to the antiwar writings of Romain Rolland and the impression made by such films as *All Quiet on the Western Front* and particularly *Kameradschaft* (*Camaraderie*), which "proclaimed the workers' solidarity across all frontiers," he acquired a "socially progressive outlook" and like Foreign Minister Aristide Briand became an advocate of Franco-German reconciliation, though without any ambition to enter actively into politics himself. Nevertheless, in 1935 he contributed a series of topical cartoons to the weekly magazine, *Vendredi*, founded by André Gide, Jean Guéhenno, and André Chamson (who were all to be authors in the wartime Editions de Minuit) in order to help promote the birth of a democratic front to ward off the perceived threat of a fascist coup in France. Having supported the Socialist-Radical-Communist Popular Front government led by Léon Blum became, indeed, one of the hallmarks of many future members of the Resistance.[14]

Although he was convinced that less harsh French treatment of the democratic Weimar Republic would have prevented the rise of Hitler to power, that unwelcome turn of events did not deter Bruller from traveling through Germany or meeting its people. While on a vacation in Switzerland he encountered an ex-German officer who "considered, as I did, that the war he had been forced to fight had been an unpardonable crime." Many of the words Vercors put into the mouth of the central character in *Le Silence de la mer* – "his love for France, his longing to see our two countries unite, and complement each other" – he had heard expressed by this man whom he later came upon, "lonely and dejected, . . . full of shame at what was happening in Germany," seated in a Parisian café en route to America as an emigré. Neither knowledge of the early Nazi concentration camps nor Hitler's aggressive foreign policy led Vercors to abandon his pacifism. During a journey across Germany in the summer of 1938 to attend the international writers' congress of the PEN club held in Prague, he allowed displays of German bonhomie viewed on station platforms and the beauty of the old medieval city of Nuremberg to efface "other, more alarming impressions" made by hard-faced officials and signs hostile to Jews. But the reluctance of the delegates forthrightly to

14. Vercors, *Battle of Silence*, pp. 14–15, 16–18; and Lottman, *Left Bank*, pp. 48–50, 76–78, 91. On the origins of the French Resistance in the spirit of the Popular Front, see Douglas Johnson, *France* (London, 1969), pp. 77–79.

condemn anti-Semitism, followed at the end of September by the Munich agreement in which France and Britain abandoned Czechoslovakia to dismemberment by Hitler, finally destroyed Bruller's faith in the principle of "peace at any price."[15] By the beginning of 1939 he had thus, at least in his mind, taken a decisive step that in the end was to lead him into the Resistance. Bruller remained in his political sympathies indisputably a *homme de gauche*, the friend of pacifist writer Jules Romains and of Communist journalist Jean-Richard Bloch, and viewed the struggle that was approaching with anguish. However, he had already broken with the powerful ideal of the Left of rapprochement between France and Germany, which enticed some French intellectuals as well as former Socialists, trade unionists, and even Communists into the ranks of the collaborators after June 1940.[16]

When war came, Bruller was called up as a reserve lieutenant. His military service was largely uneventful, except that during its course he caught his first glimpse of the "indomitable majesty" of the Vercors plateau, which henceforth exercised a growing fascination upon him. Meanwhile, after the misleading and demoralizing quiet of the "phoney war," the long-expected German assault broke over France and her hapless allies on 10 May 1940. Though not outgunned, certainly outmaneuvered and psychologically overwhelmed, they retreated and then dissolved as an effective force within five weeks. On 17 June, when the newly installed Premier Philippe Pétain informed the nation over radio that France had to cease fighting, Bruller was far from alone in being "stunned." He thought of remaining in the Vercors, perhaps joining a *maquis* or keeping a herd of cattle and in this way safeguarding "if not my freedom, at least my inner integrity." In his unit, however, to his disgust and dismay many officers – like him, all members of the

15. Konstantinović, *Vercors*, pp. 56–57; Vercors, *Battle of Silence*, pp. 19–20, 22–26, 28–29, 33–34; and *Travaux et Recherches sur la guerre: Bilan d'un séminaire, 1981–1984*, Bulletin de l'institut d'histoire du temps présent, Supplement no. 7, Serie "Seconde guerre mondiale," no. 1 ([Paris], 1985), pp. 24–26.

16. On the pacifism of interwar left-wing French intellectuals and non-Communist political organizations, and the recruits it produced for collaborationism during the German occupation, see Azéma, *From Munich to the Liberation*, pp. 3–5; Larry Ceplair, *Under the Shadow of War: Fascism, Anti-Fascism, and Marxists, 1918–1939* (New York, 1987), pp. 123–53; Cobb, *French and Germans*, pp. 89–90, 92, 112–13; Bertram M. Gordon, *Collaborationism in France during the Second World War* (Ithaca, N.Y., 1980), pp. 34–35, 38, 46; Hoffmann, *Decline or Renewal*, pp. 37ff.; and Marc Sadoun, *Les Socialistes sous l'occupation: Résistance et collaboration* (Paris, 1982), pp. 43–44.

bourgeoisie – were "full of cheer" that the war was over.[17]

Unquestionably, the vast majority of French men and women during the summer of 1940, including most intellectuals, were glad for the same reason. Those like Bruller, who vowed they would keep silent and not publish anything as long as their country remained occupied by the enemy, or like the author Jean Guéhenno, who fell back on a job as a teacher rather than write without being free, were very few. Once he had been released from the army and was able to return to Paris from the so-called *zone libre* in the south, which was ruled by Pétain's authoritarian regime headquartered at Vichy, Bruller took up work as a carpenter's apprentice in a village near the capital. His neighbors there adjusted easily to the presence of the Germans, who were not only handsome and well-behaved but who also paid for everything they needed with cash, to the delight of women and shopkeepers alike. "Oh, had it been any other war, how glad I would have been to welcome this harmony, to believe in this reconciliation." Instead, he was repelled by the sight of the first indigenous anti-Semitic journal to appear under Nazi auspices, entitled *Au Pilori*, and of Frenchmen "reduced to beasts of burden" towing Germans in bicycle-taxis; and he was humiliated by the need to obtain gas coupons and an identification card (the ubiquitous *Ausweis*) from the local *Kommandantur* in order to travel.[18] However, aside from engaging in trivial acts of sabotage, such as deliberately giving German soldiers who asked for directions on a train false information – a widespread but essentially harmless amusement among the French that came to be known as "narguer les Allemands" – and avoiding unnecessary contacts with the occupier, Bruller did not see any opportunity for more meaningful resistance. The minds of most of his countrymen "lay wrapped . . . in a tragic sleep." But

17. Vercors, *Battle of Silence*, pp. 47, 62, 67, 75, 79–80, 82–83. The vast, and largely polemical, literature dealing with the French defeat in 1940 is examined by John C. Cairns, "Along the Road Back to France 1940," *American Historical Review* 64 (1959): 583–603; see also Marc Bloch, *Strange Defeat* (London, 1949); and Guy Chapman, *Why France Collapsed* (London, 1968).

18. Vercors, *Battle of Silence*, pp. 86, 89, 92–96, 115, 122; David Pryce-Jones, *Paris in the Third Reich: A History of the German Occupation, 1940–1944* (New York, 1981), pp. 53, 103 (photograph of a "vélo-cab"); and on the violent confrontations *Au Pilori* produced between its readers and Jews, Gordon, *Collaborationism in France*, p. 87. For the attitude of the French toward the rigors of the occupation, especially food and other shortages, see Azéma, *From Munich to the Liberation*, pp. 97–103; Kedward, *Occupied France*, pp. 5–8, 14–16; and John Sweets, *Choices in Vichy France: The French under Nazi Occupation* (New York, 1986), pp. 14–17, 20–23.

how to awaken them? "I kept racking my brain: what could we do?" Pierre de Lescure cautioned him that France's struggle to escape from the abyss into which she had fallen would be a prolonged one but not to abandon hope; and Jean-Richard Bloch added encouragingly that "the battle would be resumed someday, and victoriously."[19]

In order to distract himself from the unhappiness of the present, Bruller, while still in uniform, had begun writing an account of a youthful summer romance during which he had shyly loved a girl "in silence" (she and her mother were fated to perish in Auschwitz). He continued the novel during the evenings when employed in the carpentry shop. He gradually realized, though, that earning a living for his family (he was the father of twin sons) in this manner without intending to break his silence was not an appropriate means of combatting his country's foes. An increasing number of even well-intentioned French writers and artists had resumed publishing during 1940 and 1941, including Colette, Jean Cocteau, Georges Simenon, and Jean Giraudoux, who to Bruller's chagrin had also managed the republican government's "Information Service" for a period before the armistice; their mere appearance in print was turned by the Germans into a propaganda advantage. There was a danger that others would be enticed into the same seemingly harmless behavior, since many newspapers and periodicals (particularly Drieu's *Nouvelle Revue Française*) in fact supported the Occupation while pretending to oppose it. On the other hand, in September 1940 the Publishers' Association voluntarily drew up the first of three compilations – the "liste Otto" named in honor of the recently appointed francophile German ambassador, Otto Abetz – of books by Jewish, English, Marxist, German exile, and other authors deemed unacceptable to the occupying power, which would therefore no longer be printed or sold in France. Bruller and Lescure were in agreement that a new outlet had to be found for French intellectuals to publish their work without hindrance or compromising their patriotism.[20]

19. Vercors, *Battle of Silence*, pp. 90–91, 96–97, 120–22, 140, 146; and Kedward, *Occupied France*, p. 8.
20. Vercors, *Battle of Silence*, pp. 45, 58, 70, 72, 85–86, 113, 115, 126–28, 130–34, 198–99; Konstantinović, *Vercors*, p. 57; Pryce-Jones, *Paris in the Third Reich*, pp. 26, 77, 82; and Pascal Fouché, *L'Edition française sous l'Occupation, 1940–1944* (Paris, 1987), 1:21–37, 291–347. The career of the most prominent French collaborationist writer is traced by Robert Soucy, *Fascist Intellectual: Drieu la Rochelle* (Berkeley and Los Angeles, 1979).

The immediate origins of Bruller's own literary contribution to launching this enterprise (he soon abandoned his idea of a story dealing solely with his personal experience) have been the subject of some confusion. In *The Battle of Silence* he attributed the inspiration to his discovery of a volume of memoirs about the 1940 campaign in France by a German writer. Entitled *Gärten und Straßen* (*Routes et jardins* or *Gardens and Streets*), Ernst Jünger's "very affectionate" (Bruller) recollections of the people, books, landscape, and architectural monuments he had encountered and admired during the rapid advance of his formation included numerous examples of humane treatment accorded the vanquished that did not go unappreciated by the French.

> I read this eulogy on defeated France by one of her conquerors with a feeling of profound malaise, of mounting irritation. Not that I thought it was a trap, written with ulterior motives. The author seemed quite sincere, but . . . he had been allowed to publish his book, so . . . I imagined its effect on more impressionable readers: how tempted they would be to see in this German the spokesman of what cultured Germans felt about us! A most dangerous temptation. If Jünger was not a party to this plot, he was at least its tool.[21]

However, *Gärten und Straßen* was not published until 1942, whereas the composition of *Le Silence de la mer* took place during the second half of 1941. Bruller evidently first wrote his story, then read Jünger's book and saw in it precisely the sort of German who posed a threat to France. In any case, Bruller had already met "decent" representatives of the enemy since his demobilization, in particular an officer whose troops had been temporarily quartered in his home but who had protected its furnishings with reverence and afterwards always greeted him politely on the street; he felt distinctly pained at not reciprocating this goodwill. Then he was told by a friend, a scholar of English literature who corrected his translation of Edgar Allan Poe's story "Silence," which Bruller was preparing in a limited hand-illustrated edition to sell to collectors in lieu of carpentering, about a conversation overheard in Paris between two

21. See Vercors, *Battle of Silence*, pp. 147–48; and following this account Lottman, *Left Bank*, p. 180 and, more circumspectly, Atack, *Literature and the French Resistance*, p. 64. Bruller further remarked that "Ernst Jünger loved France, but he obeyed. . . . [I]f my hero had been a man of character, he could not have been free, still less an officer"; while King described Jünger as "the Francophile who acquiesced in the virtual enslavement of France." "Language and Silence," p. 230.

Germans, a soldier and a civilian. The former warmly welcomed the prospect of France revived that a meeting and exchange of handshakes by Hitler and Pétain at Montoire-sur-le-Loir in October 1940 seemed to promise;[22] to which the other mockingly replied: "Just leave the French to lull themselves with their illusions. We must draw their claws before we destroy them. Don't you realize we're fooling them?" And he concluded by quoting Racine: "J'embrasse mon rival mais c'est pour l'étouffer" ("I embrace my rival but only to suffocate him").[23]

Thus such Germans "who loved France" and were under her spell, "who sincerely believed in a possible marriage between the two former adversaries within a happy Europe," were intended to warn "those Frenchmen who were still wavering – still deluding themselves" about the future of their country as part of the "New Order" Hitler was imposing on the European continent. Above all French writers, who like the silent girl and her uncle in the story were "almost convinced" by the beneficent demeanor of this "best possible German," should remain aloof from any form of collaboration with the occupier. As for the "hero," since neither Bruller nor most other contemporary observers could detect by mid-1941 any crack in "that vast German obedience [that] was the tragedy of their country, and of Europe as well," he could only sacrifice his life for his master, even knowing his "damnable policy."[24]

It remained to find a title "which would fit the hidden violence of

22. On the purposes and popular impact of the Montoire meetings, which publicly demonstrated the Vichy government's willingness to collaborate with Germany but which according to Vercors "had outraged the bulk of the people, as I could see even in my own village," see *Battle of Silence*, p. 118; Kedward, *Occupied France*, pp. 34–36; Paxton, *Vichy France*, pp. 74–76; and Henri Michel, *Vichy Année 40* (Paris, 1966), pp. 295–355, with a photograph of the notorious handshake following p. 336.

23. Vercors, *Battle of Silence*, pp. 81, 94–95, 120–22, 148–49, 151; Brodin, *Présences contemporaines* 1:323–24; Ernst Jünger, *Werke* (Stuttgart, 1960) 2:20, 27–230 (*Gärten und Straßen*); Hans Peter des Coudres and Horst Mühleisen, *Bibliographie der Werke Ernst Jüngers* (Stuttgart, 1985), p. 40; Bruce Chatwin, "An Aesthete at War," *New York Review of Books* (5 March 1981): 21–25; and correspondence with the editors from Dr. Liselotte Jünger and Jean Bruller, 19 January and 8 June 1990.

24. Vercors, *Battle of Silence*, pp. 149–50; see also John, "The Ambiguous Invader," p. 198; and, on the function of France as the chief economic "milch-cow" supporting Nazi imperialism after 1940, Alan S. Milward, *The New Order and the French Economy* (Oxford, 1970). As far as France's writers were concerned, the most conspicuous "good" German was Gerhard Heller, a francophile teacher of French literature in charge of the Nazi Propaganda Ministry's censorship office in Paris, who encouraged the publication of worthwhile works of literature even if they or

this tale without sound or fury. . . . Then there came to my mind a wild and poetic image which had often haunted me: beneath the deceptively calm surface of the sea, the ceaseless, cruel battles of the beasts of the deep." And so Bruller called his story *The Silence of the Sea*. His hope was that it, and books by other, established writers that might follow, would not only contribute to the slowly emerging Resistance by "safeguarding clear, accurate, persistent thinking in the face of oppression," but also thereby endure long after the war was over as lucid and intelligent works of literature. As for the imprint under which they would appear, he considered several names (for example, Underground Press, The Catacombs, Midnight Confessions) before deciding upon Editions de Minuit – Midnight Press.[25]

The actual appearance of *Le Silence de la mer*, which carried the official publishing date of 20 February 1942, was delayed for several months on account of Pierre de Lescure's concern for maintaining security in the distribution of the volumes. When in the early autumn they finally reached their audience, made up of carefully chosen literary people, artists and architects, financiers and industrialists, elementary and secondary schoolteachers, lawyers and judges, medical doctors, professors, scientists and technicians residing in both zones (as well as Drieu la Rochelle and Ambassador Abetz), each copy carried a statement Lescure had drafted on the ideals of the new undertaking. After pointing out that "today the physics of Einstein, the psychology of Freud, and the book of Isaiah are banned," and that French publishers and booksellers had similarly removed all objectionable authors from their catalogues and windows, the manifesto recalled earlier periods in the history of France when "writers who refused to praise their masters" had been eliminated. "In France there still are some writers . . . who refuse to obey orders. They feel that they must express themselves. To influence others, perhaps, but above all because if they don't express themselves the mind will die." He concluded that the aim

---

their authors were politically suspect and whom François Mauriac explicitly identified with the German officer in *Le Silence de la mer*. Jacques Debû-Bridel, ed., *La Résistance intellectuelle: Textes et témoignages* (Paris, 1970), p. 100; Cobb, *French and Germans*, p. 58; Lottman, *Left Bank*, pp. 144, 174–79; and Pryce-Jones, *Paris in the Third Reich*, pp. 249–52.

25. Vercors, *Battle of Silence*, pp. 153, 155–56, 165–67. Bruller added the brief explanation on the symbolic meaning he was evoking when the printer Oudeville asked why the story was not entitled *"The Silence of the Niece."*

of the Editions de Minuit was to protect "our inner life and serve our art in freedom." For that, names and personal reputations were unimportant. "It is a matter of man's spiritual purity."[26]

The lengthy period between the conception in June 1941 and the actual circulation of Vercors's book led Yvonne Paraf to fear that it might be "dated." And, indeed, the heightened brutality the war evinced, especially following the invasion of Russia and the onset of the Holocaust perpetrated against European Jewry, made the story appear almost idyllic to some readers. Nevertheless, it still represented a principled appeal to French men and women to shun any form of a modus vivendi with even the least hateful of the German occupiers, an attitude that the bulk of the population came to adopt during the course of 1942.[27] A second edition of *Le Silence de la mer* was therefore soon called for; it carried the imprint "25 July 1943, the day of the overthrow of Rome's tyrant" (that is, Fascist dictator Benito Mussolini). However, Vercors realized it was imperative for the young undertaking to publish another volume promptly if it was to demonstrate abroad "the existence in captive France of a vast national movement of thought opposed to the Nazi stranglehold." His attention focused on a text by the exiled Catholic philosopher Jacques Maritain entitled *A travers le désastre* (*Through the Disaster*), which after its appearance in America had been smuggled into the *zone libre* where it was reprinted. Vercors decided to make the hazardous crossing of the demarcation line both to secure the manuscript for the Editions de Minuit and to organize the distribution network in the south. After considerable difficulty even in obtaining a copy of Maritain's little book, Oudeville arranged for it to be run off using a linotype machine, which was an easier process than the one used to produce its predecessor. It was paid for by a contribution of five thousand francs (Vercors: "a tidy sum") from Professor Robert Debré, a distinguished pediatrician and member of the French Academy of Medicine who later belonged to the directing council of the National Front, the main Communist-dominated Resistance organization. The firm's second title was therefore published on 12 November 1942, the day after

26. Ibid., pp. 172, 174–76, 178, 182, 190, 199, 202; Debû-Bridel, *Les Editions de Minuit*, p. 94; Jean Paulhan and Dominique Aury, *La Patrie se fait tous les jours: Textes français, 1939–1945* (Paris, 1947), pp. 121–22; and Germaine Brée and George Bernauer, eds., *Defeat and Beyond: An Anthology of French Wartime Writing, 1940–1945* (New York, 1970), pp. 247–48.

27. John, "The Ambiguous Invader," pp. 197–98; see also Sweets, *Choices in Vichy France*, pp. 118, 131–36, 168–69, 175, 192, 208–9.

the Germans, in the wake of the Anglo-American landings in French North Africa, extended their occupation to all of metropolitan France.[28]

Vercors was still not satisfied, though, with the pace of publication. Over a year had passed since he had finished composing his story, and no other suitable manuscript from a writer living in France had come to his attention. An overture during his southern trip to Roger Martin du Gard, in the hope that greatly respected novelist might furnish the Editions de Minuit with something, was graciously yet firmly rebuffed. Nor had Jean Paulhan, the head of the prominent Gallimard publishing company who until displaced by Drieu la Rochelle had edited the *Nouveile Revue Française* and still the acknowledged "pope of French literature" (Vercors), been successful in locating a text, as Lescure through a middleman had requested he attempt. This individual was the writer Jacques Debû-Bridel; an employee of the Ministry of Marine, he was secretly passing information on movements of the French fleet in the Mediterranean to England. Then suddenly, at the beginning of 1943, Paulhan himself and Debû-Bridel along with Yvonne Paraf and Vercors all submitted short pieces of work that were brought out together in April of that year. Paulhan's contribution was an appreciation of the writings of Jacques Decour, the Communist editor of *La Pensée libre* shot by the Germans in 1942, while Yvonne "Desvignes" presented an essay on the need for *L'Indignation*. From Debû-Bridel came *Pages de journal*, containing his devastating critique of the defeatist French press during the 1940 campaign. An anonymous poem dealt with the hated *Relève*, the Vichy government's scheme to supply workers to German industry as substitutes for French prisoners of war held by the enemy. In his novella *Désespoir est mort*, which appeared under the pseudonym Santerre in order "to make us look more numerous" (at Yvonne Paraf's suggestion, all of the pen names used were henceforth those of French provinces), Vercors rejected despair as a solution even to the sorry condition in which his country then found itself. And his unsigned verse "Les Morts" commemorated the thousands upon thousands of "Russians, Jews, women, children" who had so far lost their lives in the war. A final item in the collection, *Le Rapport d'Uriel* by the aging philosopher Julian Benda (the author in 1927 of the

28. Vercors, *Battle of Silence*, pp. 175, 180, 182, 184–96, 199–200, 202, 210, 229; Debû-Bridel, *Les Éditions de Minuit*, pp. 37–38, 93; and Paulhan and Aury, *La Patrie se fait tous les jours*, pp. 279–84.

programmatic study *The Treason of the Intellectuals*), was a dryly humorous treatment of his perennial *bête noir*, the German nation. This "honorable though somewhat slender" volume under the title *Chroniques interdites* (*The Forbidden Chronicles*) was printed in 1,500 copies, three or four times the size of the first edition of *Le Silence de la mer* and of Maritain's book.[29]

This extravagance had been made possible by Ernest Aulard's decision to take over the task of printing from Oudeville: working on Sundays behind closed shutters with only two trusted employees, using a much larger press, and burning any waste paper to allay suspicion before the rest of the personnel arrived in the shop Monday morning. However, binding and distributing so many volumes created serious logistical difficulties. Aulard solved the one problem when he found a reliable professional bookbinder who worked alone at home, Vercors the other by enlisting the help of Ceux de la Résistance (Those of the Resistance Movement) through an acquaintance who headed it to transport books to its own members. The editor of *Les Lettres françaises*, Claude Morgan, arranged for distribution in Communist networks. Establishing connections with important Resistance organizations marked the acceptance of the publishing enterprise as an integral part of the nationwide opposition against the occupying power. Its worth was attested by the fact that the Organisation Civile et Militaire, another leading Resistance group, offered to provide a subsidy of 50,000 francs if future publications would include an acknowledgment of this (Vercors declined on the ground that this would compromise the independence of the undertaking).[30] Even more valuable, such recognition meant that manuscripts began to arrive in increasing numbers and from well-known writers, indeed the élite of the French literary world. During the final year preceding the liberation, the firm was able to publish over thirty additional

29. Vercors, *Battle of Silence*, pp. 171–72, 181–82, 193, 200, 210–13; see also Vercors, "Désespoir est mort," reprinted in *Le Silence de la mer et autres récits* (Paris, 1951), pp. 7–20; Vercors, "Les Morts," reprinted in Pierre Seghers, *La Résistance et ses poètes: France, 1940/1945*, 3rd. rev. ed. (Paris, 1974), pp. 635–37; and Jacques Debû-Bridel ("Argonne"), "Pages from a Diary," translated in Liebling, ed., *Republic of Silence*, pp. 21–26. Julian Benda once remarked that "the Middle Ages had the Plague, the Twentieth Century has the Germans." David L. Schalk, *The Spectrum of Political Engagement* (Princeton, N.J., 1979), p. 131.

30. Vercors, *Battle of Silence*, pp. 212–17, 219, 232, 234, 242–43; also Kedward, *Occupied France*, p. 49. For the same reason Vercors later turned down a similar offer from a Gaullist representative.

texts. They comprised a wide range of works of prose and poetry, fiction and contemporary history, philosophy and political thought. Among the authors and their writings that appeared under the imprint of the Editions de Minuit until the end of July 1944 (the last volumes were hawked over the barricades that went up in Paris in anticipation of the arrival of Allied and Free French forces) were Elsa Triolet's *Les Amants d'Avignon*, the story by the companion of Louis Aragon of a female liaison agent; Aragon's own anti-German *Le Musée grévin* and *Le Crime contre l'esprit* (the former included the poem "Auschwitz," the latter a dramatic account of the personalities and fate of one of the earliest Resistance circles at the Parisian Musée de l'Homme); by France's other great Communist poet, Paul Eluard, who replaced Lescure as the principal literary figure in the enterprise, *L'Honneur des poètes* and *Europe*, two collections of his own and others' poems (among them verses of unidentified writers probably killed in the Resistance and by non-French opponents of fascism); *Contes d'Auxois* by the journalist Edith Thomas, short stories about acts of resistance; from François Mauriac, the only member of the French Academy who rallied unequivocally to the Resistance, meditations on the state of France and Europe in *Le Cahier noir*; André Gide's *Fragments d'un journal*, on the liberation of Tunis (to where he had retired midway through the war) at the hands of the Allies; and by the steadfast Jean Guéhenno, *Dans la prison*, a vivid memoir of life in occupied France. Perhaps the most remarkable book, *33 sonnets* by Jean Cassou, consisted of poems he had composed while incarcerated but could only commit to paper after his release. From America came John Steinbeck's inspiring tale of Resistance in Norway, *The Moon Is Down* (translated by Yvonne Paraf and published as *Nuits noires* in February 1944).[31] And there was a volume that combined selections from the writings of the Communist martyr Gabriel Péri and the Catholic philosopher Charles Péguy, intended both to demonstrate the common humanity of Resistance thinking and to

31. Vercors, *Battle of Silence*, pp. 220–21, 224–27, 231, 235–36, 247–51, 256–58, 276; see also Azéma, *From Munich to the Liberation*, pp. 158, 255; Seghers, *La Résistance et ses poètes*, pp. 267–68; Lottman, *Left Bank*, p. 193; Atack, *Literature and the French Resistance*, pp. 90–93, 109–13, 142–45; Brée and Bernauer, eds., *Defeat and Beyond*, pp. 62–68, 204–11, 224–30; Liebling, ed., *Republic of Silence*, pp. 158–70; and Paulhan and Aury, *La Patrie se fait tous les jours*, pp. 195–97, 307–14, 375–78. Steinbeck's somewhat lengthier volume, which required more time (and hence entailed greater danger) to print, appeared in a large and – unlike an earlier Swiss-French – unexpurgated edition, for which effort and risk the author was to

rescue the latter author from misleading exploitation at the hands of Vichy propagandists.[32]

Vercors's decision not to publish most of his newer writing until after the war was over reflected, in part, a significant transformation in his attitude toward the occupier. Contrary to the views of many Resistance leaders, as late as 1943 he persisted in distinguishing between "Germans," on the one hand, and "Nazis," on the other. At that time he maintained that "the old Germany of Kant and the humanists" had not been wholly destroyed by Hitler, and he was prepared to accept texts for publication in the Editions de Minuit from exiles like Thomas Mann or Bertolt Brecht should they be offered to him. However, as the incidence and severity of crimes perpetrated against the French and other peoples by the Occupation forces mounted, Vercors's ideal of detachment from daily events in the interest of preserving "clear, dispassionate thought" began to change. In a short novel entitled *Les Mots* (*The Words*) – it finally appeared only in 1947 – he told the story of a poet who sought isolation from the world but instead was witness to the destruction of a village and the killing of its inhabitants, which led him to cry out in horror for vengeance; and yet a mere kilometer of distance might have spared him this sight and so enabled him to continue composing his "words" in peace. But, Vercors asked, would a writer who in these circumstances was unwilling to sacrifice his serene independence from the affairs of the world not be behaving as a traitor to mankind "without whom there is no poetry"? In the case of his essay "Le Songe" ("The Dream"), which recounted information obtained from an ex-inmate of Oranienburg concentration camp about the slow extermination of the prisoners there, he preferred to withhold it from publication rather than further distress the relatives of those deported to such places. Although he found it difficult to believe the worst reports of the death factories because they were reminiscent of the discredited propaganda tales of the First World War, eventually Vercors had to accept the fact of Nazism's degradation of men from civilization to barbarity. This recognition brought him to loathe Germans without differentiation; he did not even feel pity at their losses when the

---

show himself callously ungrateful: "one of our first and greatest postwar disappointments" (Vercors).

32. See Vercors's own tribute to Péri in *Portrait d'une amitié*, pp. 111–15; also Werth, *France, 1940–1955*, pp. 42–43, on the selective enlistment of the nationalist Péguy "as a sort of ideological saint of Pétainism."

beaten *Wehrmacht* retreated from the soil of France. He was ashamed, though, of such emotions in himself and hated the enemy all the more for having aroused them: "I knew that in this sense the Nazis would remain victorious, even after their defeat and disappearance."[33]

By the spring of 1944, the Editions de Minuit was established on a virtually unshakeable basis. The contact with *Les Lettres françaises* placed a second printer at the firm's disposal. Gaullists in London obtained copies of *Le Silence de la mer* and other of its publications, and Vercors's story in miniature format was scattered by air drops all over the country. They even decided to reprint them abroad under the label "Les Cahiers du silence." Some volumes also appeared in Switzerland. Meanwhile, separate series of factual and of foreign books, called "Témoignages" ("Bearing Witness") and "Voix d'outre-monde" ("Voices from Another World") respectively, were started. The former included the first serious document to circulate in occupied territory on the events behind the 1940 armistice as well as a truthful account of the scuttling of the French fleet at Toulon after German entry into the *zone libre*. Various Parisian booksellers surreptitiously stocked titles at the risk of their lives. The distribution system elsewhere functioned efficiently; nor were finances a problem: there was a subscription service, and those left over were sold among the Resistance groups. Only members of the *maquis* actively engaged in fighting received free copies. Profits were intended for distribution after the war to the needy families of printers who had been executed or imprisoned. Eluard, Debû-Bridel, Vercors, Claude Morgan, and two or three others sat on an editorial board that met weekly in Yvonne Paraf's apartment to decide the order in which the numerous manuscripts on hand would be published. After the Allied landing in Normandy on 6 June, there was agreement that all efforts by the Resistance henceforth should be concentrated upon military operations; for that reason, only those texts already received and being

33. Vercors, *Battle of Silence*, pp. 215, 226, 259–62, 277–78, 282; Vercors, "Le Songe," reprinted in *Le Silence de la mer et autres récits*, pp. 95–112; Konstantinović, *Vercors*, p. 196; Atack, *Literature and the French Resistance*, pp. 100–102; John, "The Ambiguous Invader," pp. 197–99; Wilkinson, *Intellectual Resistance*, p. 176; and Konrad F. Bieber, *L'Allemagne vue par les écrivains de la Résistance française* (Geneva and Lille, 1954), pp. 123–46; see also Sweets, *Choices in Vichy France*, pp. 189–91, for evidence of a similar change in attitude among the French in general, so that by 1944 many refused any longer to distinguish between "good" Germans and "bad" Nazis as some major Resistance newspapers still attempted to do.

set would still appear in print. An advertisement for these was even slipped into the final issue of the official *Bibliographie de la France* that came out before the liberation.[34]

Had it been up to Vercors, the Editions de Minuit would have closed down and he himself would have remained in anonymity after the war ended. The business lacked capital and its leading figures were not publishers by profession; he feared it would not be long before they lost control over the enterprise. From his earliest association with it, however, Debû-Bridel for one had glimpsed in the undertaking an organ for the entire Resistance to perpetuate its ideals against the great majority of the industry that had signed the "Otto list." That viewpoint prevailed, and so the firm continued for a few years as Aux Editions de Minuit, reprinting its wartime volumes as well as bringing out new ones on the Resistance by its established authors or survivors of Nazi persecution. But by 1948 the harsh realities of postwar austerity forced it to pass into other hands.[35]

As for Vercors, he had been deeply impressed by the spirit of self-sacrifice, dedication, and loyalty prevailing among his erstwhile comrades in arms; notwithstanding the bereavement and anguish they regularly had to bear, he confessed "how happy we had been." No single political group during the Occupation suffered heavier casualties than the Communists, the "party of the *fusillés*." Unlike General de Gaulle (whose acquaintance he made immediately after Paris was liberated), Vercors did not regard its adherents as lacking in patriotism toward France when they also served another cause. Therefore, without ever becoming a member of the PCF, he joined Cassou as well as Aragon – and just about everyone else who wrote for the Resistance – on the Communist-dominated National Committee of Writers (CNE). Its first self-appointed task in 1945 was to purge French literary life of collaborationist and fascist influences. But as time passed, the organization and others to

34. Vercors, *Battle of Silence*, pp. 218–24, 230, 243, 247–49, 254–55, 257–58, 269, 274; Atack, *Literature and the French Resistance*, pp. 5, 12; Fouché, *L'Edition française sous l'Occupation* 2:160; and Seghers, *La Résistance et ses poètes*, p. 266. Vercors had quarreled with Pierre de Lescure, who left Paris to join the *maquis* and thereby withdrew from participation in the publishing enterprise.

35. Vercors, *Battle of Silence*, pp. 181–82, 272; Sweets, *Politics of Resistance*, pp. 111, 221; Liebling, ed., *Republic of Silence*, p. 183; Lottman, *Left Bank*, p. 232; and Germaine Brée, *Twentieth-Century French Literature* (Chicago, 1983), pp. 72, 75–76, 280. The new owners, who carried on the name, combined political with literary engagement, and the firm published many avant-garde French as well as foreign authors including Alain Robbe-Grillet and Samuel Beckett.

which Vercors belonged or (in the case of the CNE) even headed and whose congresses he dutifully attended increasingly became mere mouthpieces for Moscow's policies during the Cold War confrontation with the United States. One by one, the "fellow travelers" dropped away, whether over the issue of Tito's heretical demand for Yugoslavian national independence or of the continued existence of slave labor camps and anti-Semitism in the Soviet Union. After futile attempts to distinguish his goals of world peace and international fellowship from those of the party, Vercors along with such intellectuals as Jean-Paul Sartre and Simone de Beauvoir in 1956 issued a strong denunciation of Russia's suppression of the Hungarian uprising. With that, his flirtation with Communism was over: the "decorative vase," as he described his rôle, was "no longer presentable."[36] Otherwise, he went on pursuing the writing career begun in the Resistance. His productivity, which ranged over novels, plays, essays, children's books, and most recently historical works, varied from period to period; nevertheless, his reputation as an author has grown to the point where he is considered a possible nominee for the Nobel Prize in literature.[37]

Should that honor be accorded Vercors, it is safe to surmise that it would recognize first and foremost his unique contribution to the intellectual Resistance in France both as writer and publisher. But what impact did that phenomenon have upon the country's wartime experience, and within it what precisely was the significance of Vercors, *Le Silence de la mer*, and the Editions de Minuit? Some observers have denied the efficacy of any such oppositional activities: "How could words help when a brutal enemy occupied one's soil?" Ambassador Abetz, on the other hand, argued that since

36. Vercors, *Battle of Silence*, pp. 272–73, 284–86; see also Werth, *France, 1940–1955*, p. 196; Wilkinson, *Intellectual Resistance*, pp. 50, 76, 78–79; Ilya Ehrenburg, *Men, Years – Life* (Cleveland and New York, 1966), 6:140; Charles de Gaulle, *Lettres, notes et carnets, juin 1951–mai 1958*, (Paris, 1985), 7:268–69, 348; Noguères, *Histoire de la Résistance* 1:437–38; Johnson, *France*, p. 163; Novick, *Resistance versus Vichy*, pp. 126–29; Lottman, *Left Bank*, pp. 220–24, 254–55, 262, 266, 269–71, 286–87; Brée, *Twentieth–Century French Literature*, p. 348; Fouché, *L'Edition française sous l'Occupation* 2:167, 190–93, 220–23; and Caute, *Fellow-Travellers*, pp. 103, 198–99, 212, 285–87, 289, 291, 356–57. David Caute's description of Vercors as a "Donald Duck" who for years managed to shake off his misgivings about Soviet behavior, underestimates the profound indebtedness he felt toward the *résistants* in the ranks of the PCF – and to the Red Army – for France's liberation from Nazi tyranny.

37. Metzger, ed., *Contemporary Authors* 12:92–93; Brodin, *Présences contemporaines* 1:327–31; and information from Professor Jack Kolbert, 23 February 1987. (Note: Jean Bruller died at his home in Paris on 10 June 1991, in his eighty-ninth year.)

France's output of books during the war actually surpassed the level of both America and England, French cultural and scientific activity had not been impeded by the occupying power (and hence, by implication, intellectual Resistance against it was unnecessary and ineffective).[38] Indeed, even Sartre, who explicitly rejected collaboration with the Germans, found no difficulty having his work performed and acclaimed, including the 1943 drama *Les Mouches* (*The Flies*), which was intended to be anti-Nazi in tone.[39] Yet in a land where language is identified with national survival – an attitude summarized in the title of an essay by one Resistance writer, "Ma patrie, la langue française" – the decision of just a handful of authors not to publish anything until France was completely free alone guaranteed the preservation of her particular cultural values. This abstinence was all the more vital as the full implications of Nazi rule for French sovereignty became apparent and when the designated protector of the nation's spiritual existence, the Académie Française, with the single exception of Mauriac (and, to a lesser degree, Georges Duhamel) either supported the Pétainist regime or cooperated enthusiastically with enemy propaganda efforts.[40] Whereas these encompassed art, theater, and films as well as literature,[41] the intellectual Resistance had at its disposal only one weapon – the printed page.

Although Jean Bruller was not the sole Frenchman who in 1940

38. See Lottman, *Left Bank*, pp. 152–53, 194; and Brée, *Twentieth–Century French Literature*, pp. 67–70. Although Abetz's statistics do not always coincide with those from official publishing–trade sources, there can be no question than book production in France – especially during the years 1942–44 – was notably high.

39. The philosopher, who soon after the liberation wrote movingly of the severe tribulations his countrymen underwent during the Occupation, was also candid enough to admit upon reflection: "I wonder if I shall be understood if I say that it was both intolerable and at the same time we put up with it very well." Sartre, "The Republic of Silence," in Liebling, ed., *Republic of Silence* pp. 498–500; and Azéma, *From Munich to the Liberation*, p. 96.

40. King, "Language and Silence," pp. 227–28, 237; Novick, *Resistance versus Vichy*, pp. 129–30; and Werth, *France, 1940–1955*, pp. 44–45. Duhamel, the first writer Vercors approached to contribute to *La Pensée libre*, declined on account of its Communist connection as well as his preference to work instead to prevent a complete Nazi takeover of the Academy. Vercors, *Battle of Silence*, pp. 135–36.

41. Though only a few French motion pictures produced during the war were explicitly collaborationist (and these, like Nazi imports, attracted small audiences), many well-known actors and actresses, artists, and writers unquestioningly accepted German patronage by traveling to cultural events and sites in the Reich. See Vercors, *Battle of Silence*, p. 235; Azéma, *From Munich to the Liberation*, pp. 94, 96–97, 233; Lottman, *Left Bank*, pp. 169–71; and Cobb, *French and Germans*, pp. 80–83.

chose to keep silent rather than bestow any comfort upon the occupier through word or deed, his novel was the first written expression of the meaning of such behavior. For two years no book had appeared in France without the stamp of the German censor. Its publication therefore created a sensation, despite the fact that the 250 to 350 copies of the original edition were miniscule in comparison to the most popular collaborationist writing.[42] By mid-1943, however, "everybody" in Paris was talking about *Le Silence de la mer* (albeit "practically nobody" yet had been able to read it); before the war ended the number in circulation, some mimeographed or handwritten, was beyond counting.[43] Vercors and his story thus came to symbolize intellectual Resistance to Nazism. They exactly captured the mood of the French with the Germans, both good and bad, in their midst, while furnishing guidance to the vanquished on how they ought to treat the conquerors.[44] The more than two dozen attractively printed and bound little books that followed in editions of one or two thousand constituted a library of some of the country's foremost authors. From them readers learned less about the day-to-day course of events – for that there was the underground press, which in 1944 appeared regularly in several hundred thousand issues – than of the overriding philosophical questions the struggle raised among the best minds in France and abroad. But their morale, too, was raised: "We should feel honored," Guéhenno wrote in his diary *Dans la prison*. "A tyrannical power,

42. Recollections about the exact size of the first edition of *Le Silence de la mer* vary somewhat; but in any case Lucien Rebatet's 1942 chronicle of France's "betrayal" by republicans and Jews that culminated in her military defeat by Germany, *Les Décombres* (*The Ruins*), sold 1,500 copies signed by the author the day it was published, 50,000 within a year, and despite paper rationing 250,000 before the war ended. See Lottman, *Left Bank*, p. 182; Henry Noguères and others, *Histoire de la Résistance en France de 1940 à 1945* (Paris, 1969), vol. 2, *L'Armée de l'ombre Juillet 1941–Octobre 1942*, pp. 351–52; S.B. John, "Vichy France, 1940–1944: The Literary Image," in John Cruickshank, ed., *French Literature and its Background* (London, 1970), vol. 6, *The Twentieth Century*, p. 213; Wilkinson, *Intellectual Resistance*, pp. 41, 287; and Pryce-Jones, *Paris in the Third Reich*, p. 63.

43. Vercors, *Battle of Silence*, p. 229; Lottman, *Left Bank*, p. 184; Charles de Gaulle, *War Memoirs* (London, 1959), vol. 2, *Unity, 1942–1944*, p. 175; and Bliven, "Keeping a Secret," p. 204.

44. Sartre, *What is Literature?*, p. 53; also Liebling, ed., *Republic of Silence*, p. 171; and John, "The Ambiguous Invader," pp. 195, 197–98. The steadily increasing interest the book aroused in metropolitan France as well as overseas, to which the (admittedly imprecise) statistics on circulation attested, contradict both the view of Sartre that by 1943 it "had lost its effectiveness" and that of S.B. John that its chief character is "frankly implausible . . . not believable."

by attributing so much importance to our thoughts, obliges us to recognize how untoward and irrepressible they are. It gives us back to ourselves. We did not dare to believe we were so important."[45] In fact, while the political influence these *intellectuels engagés* exercised upon their fellow citizens can only be surmised, it seems certain that the Nazis took them seriously. Nevertheless, thanks to the strict security precautions Lescure initiated and Vercors (whose own identity was known to no more than three people) imposed upon the authors of the Editions de Minuit, not one of them fell victim to the Gestapo; because his distinctive literary style threatened to betray him, Mauriac was simply obliged to go into hiding.[46] On the eve of the liberation Goebbels's Paris-based Propaganda Office, in desperation, was preparing to undermine the reputation of the enterprise by distributing under a bogus imprint some 80,000 copies of a collection of alleged prophecies "full of dark hints of Britain's imminent doom" and the like. This bizarre plot was stillborn.[47] And so *Les Lettres françaises* could praise the publishing venture as "an affirmation of the tenacity and will to live of the French spirit." Its most characteristic statement, "compelling in its simplicity" and still after almost fifty years (contrary to Sartre's prediction) exciting to read,[48] has become the single work of literature by a contemporary that best reflects the state of France at the moment of her greatest crisis.

45. Lottman, *Left Bank*, pp. 183–84; Azéma, *From Munich to the Liberation*, p. 157; Liebling, ed., *Republic of Silence*, p. 165; and Henri Michel, *Bibliographie critique de la Résistance* (Paris, 1964), p. 22.
46. Lottman, *Left Bank*, p. 184; and King, "Language and Silence," p. 235. The statement by Milton Dank, *The French against the French: Collaboration and Resistance* (Philadelphia, 1974), p. 179, that "the Gestapo never seems to have paid much attention to the Editions de Minuit" because only one of its authors was killed, is doubly misleading: the Communist scholar and novelist Jacques Decour was instead the editor of *La Pensée libre* and its successor journal, *Les Lettres françaises*, and was arrested (and later shot as a hostage) because of the inadequate measures taken to protect these undertakings, from which the founders of the "Editions de Minuit" learned their lesson. See Azéma, *From Munich to the Liberation*, pp. 152, 255; and Vercors, *Battle of Silence*, p. 154.
47. Vercors, *Battle of Silence*, pp. 267–68; and Fouché, *L'Edition française sous l'Occupation* 2:61. It foundered on an error involving the Germans' own regulations and French law: the volumes were stamped with too low a censorship number to be sold convincingly!
48. Sartre, *What is Literature?*, p. 54; and Wilkinson, *Intellectual Resistance*, pp. 44–45. More than a million copies of *Le Silence de la mer* have been published in numerous editions and languages worldwide. See Konstantinović, *Vercors*, p. 67; and information supplied to the editors by Jean Bruller.

Literary Introduction
James W. Brown

When men can no longer love and work singing their joy for life, they slave away silently, ferociously at terrible deeds that, one day, will liberate them. Great revolutions are elaborated in silence and rich thoughts and works germinate, far from all the noise and chatter.

— Jacques Debû–Bridel

Le Silence de la mer. How enigmatic this title, how rich with ambiguity. Not so, of course, if one seeks facile and convenient explanations, for Vercors himself points out the ostensibly paradoxical nature of calm surfaces and tumultuous depths:

I took a long time trying to find a title which would fit the hidden violence of this tale without sound or fury. Every day I lined up scores of them but found none to my liking. Then there came to my mind a wild and poetic image which had often haunted me: beneath the deceptively calm surface of the sea, the ceaseless, cruel battles of the beasts of the deep. And I called my story *The Silence of the Sea.*[1]

The metaphor is hardly original, one of its most eloquent spokesmen being the character Lorenzaccio in Musset's famous play of the same title.[2] And certainly, even within the confines of French

1. Vercors, *Battle of Silence*, p. 153 (hereafter cited in the text as Vercors, *Battle*).
2. The theme of the underside of life was quite common in nineteenth-century French literature. It was frequently illustrated in Balzac's portraits of the Parisian underworld wherein the reader is made to perceive the world as it is, not as it appears. Imagistically speaking, it took on several forms: for Balzac, Paris was *l'Enfer;* for Victor Hugo and Emile Zola, gastro-alimentary imagery symbolized the unseen machinations of a corrupt society; and, for Musset, as for Vercors, it was reflected in the tumultuous occurrences beneath the surface of the sea:

Vous étiez plein de confiance dans l'ouvrage de Dieu. Mais moi, pendant ce temps-là, j'ai plongé; je me suis enfoncé dans cette mer houleuse de la vie; j'en ai parcouru toutes les profondeurs, couvert de ma cloche de verre; tandis que vous admiriez la surface, j'ai vu les débris des naufrages, les ossements et les Léviathans. (Alfred de Musset, *Lorenzaccio* [Paris: Nouveaux Classiques Larousse, 1971], p. 90)

Finally, Rimbaud's famous poem "Bateau Ivre" is perhaps the most complete expansion on this theme in all of French literature.

literature alone, the theme of silence has attracted such notable figures as Pascal, "The eternal silence of these infinite spaces frightens me"; Vigny, "Only silence is great: all the rest is weakness"; and Stendhal, "The executioner strangled Cardinal Carafa with a silk cord that broke. He had to try it a second time. The cardinal looked at the executioner without deigning to say a word." It would be pointless to cite further French authors who for one reason or another have exploited the theme of silence. Let it suffice to say that its meaning depends somewhat on the context in which it appears. In the case of Vercors's novella, one may describe its significance as being both historical (silence as resistance) and literary (silence as sign). This introduction examines the symbolic function of silence primarily as a literary device. In attempting to delve into the depths of *Le Silence de la mer*, one is confronted with some important questions: How deeply do we go into this theme? And how far do we extend our exploration laterally, that is in directions that take us outside of the text into history and biography? How do we add something new to a theme, a work, that has already received an enormous amount of critical commentary? How do we do justice to this theme as it appears in Vercors's text itself or, more accurately, as it operates in the text? Perhaps the key word in answering the foregoing questions is "operates." By changing critical perspectives slightly, we may actually be able to perceive *Le Silence de la mer* in a new light. Rather than ask the hackneyed question, What does silence mean? which amounts to interpreting a text whose possible meanings have practically been exhausted, what if we were to ask; What is its capacity to signify? This latter approach, while not eschewing biographical and historical aspects of the story, allows us to frame them in a purely literary cadre and also permits us to see how, in a silent world, communication is achieved.

The silence of the sea. A silence that hides something, a silence charged with an undisclosed intensity; an energy in reserve, awaiting release, wanting to surface. Silence has many facets, perhaps an infinite number of facets, for being the domain of the unsaid, the nonarticulated, it is a semantic slot, a space waiting to be filled with meaning. Writers more than anyone are aware of the creative powers of silence, the wellspring of the word, and Vercors more than any of his fellow resistance authors has exploited the awesome potential of a silence used to communicate. Paradoxical as it may appear, communication is precisely what silence aims at, and it is no coincidence that writers during the early war years used silence to transmit messages of different sorts – Resistance, naturally, but also moral, philosophical and ideological ones – to their compatriots as well as to the Nazis, as we shall see shortly.

Vercors had been sensitive to the aesthetic and emotional world of silence well before finding a title for his story. As stated in the Historical Introduction, he had been playing with the ramifications of the word *silence* while illustrating three poetic tales by Edgar Allan Poe, and although he denies any direct connection between his amplification of the theme in his novella and his personal experience of its delicate powers, resonances of its nuances during a summer romance with an adolescent girl named Stéphanie can be felt in the nascent love between the German officer, von Ebrennac, in *Le Silence de la mer* and the narrator's niece.

From another angle as well, silence imposed itself upon Vercors's consciousness, for he was an engraver by profession. The world of the visual artist is one in which the work unfolds silently. Color, form, shape, texture – these are the words of the artist. In Gestalt terms, silence is the ground, the blank, empty canvas upon which the work is framed. It is not only a modus operandi for an artist, but also a modus vivendi. From within this muted space the world is perceived, even conceived, and it is certainly not fortuitous that the form Vercors's novella would take, its narrative techniques and trajectory, grew more out of his vocation as a writer.

Then, of course, there were the historical events and realities surrounding Vercors at the time of the novel's conception: his waning pacifism, the German assault on France in 1940 and the subsequent Occupation, the emerging Resistance and, most importantly, silence as a form of opposition. It is perhaps this latter theme that has attracted the attention of the vast majority of critics and commentators on *Le Silence de la mer*. Several penetrating critical and historical accounts of the roles and functions of silence–qua–resistance have appeared over the years, yet no one has examined how silence actually functions and signifies within the text itself. Rather, the theme is usually treated extratextually, in its historical, social, and moral implications. Vercors himself, in recounting French attitudes about silence during the Occupation, sums up this position and its importance for French intellectuals: "When the Nazis occupied France after the defeat of 1940, French writers had two alternatives: collaboration or silence" (Vercors, *Battle*, p. 11). Similarly, the word haunted him as he worked on his last album of etchings before the war broke out: "It was as if, with this word [silence], I had meant to strike the three taps to signal the rise of the curtain on the long tragedy which France, gagged, was to live through, in effect, in silence" (Vercors, *Battle*, p. 15). For French writers, there was only one law according to Vercors: to keep silent. Yet, paradoxically, he and others also felt the need to "lift the lid of silence" and to speculate on the question of whether silence was indeed a means of doing battle.

In a very sensitive appraisal of the question, Jacques Debû–Bridel outlines the contours of the significance of silence. In the first place, he speaks of that " . . . silence which had its own eloquence by signifying refusal."[3] This "silence du mépris," he says, was the most formidable weapon of French writers in the occupied zone. On the other hand, he states: "Silence is an avowal of impotence, of defeat, but at the same a safeguard and a refuge of the vanquished." (Debû–Bridel, *Résistance*, p. 39). A silence that denies, a silence that admits defeat. Such a position is untenable even though it reveals a certain pride in the affirmation of refusal. Debû–Bridel clearly recognized the need for writers to overcome this phase of linguistic impotence, to transform it into an act: "Silence is a costume of mourning, it affirms. It thus signifies to a triumphant Caesar in such or such a circumstance the very limit of his triumph, the nonacquiescence of the vanquished to his victory. It is already more than a symbol, it becomes an act, it is a part of the battle." (Debû-Bridel, *Résistance*, p. 40).

Another historical perspective on the dynamics of silence is offered by J.H. King. He restates some of Debû–Bridel's themes of silence as a refusal to write, as a form of passive resistance, as "a kind of primordial value," but goes one step further in underscoring " . . . a silence which, like that of the sea, conceals a clandestine activity, a secret life, a silence which protects certain values, not a silence which is merely evidence of resignation."[4] It is the motif of protection that is especially revealing because it bespeaks, in the final analysis, a contradictory position vis-à-vis European civilization and values. On the one hand, there exists the paradox of the writer who has become voluntarily silent. His word is his breath: without it, he suffocates, yet as Debû–Bridel querried: "Of what

3. Jacques Debû-Bridel, ed., *La Résistance intellectuelle* (Paris, 1970), p. 37 (hereafter cited in the text as Debû-Bridel, *Résistance*).
4. J.H. King, "Language and Silence," p. 229 (hereafter cited in the text as King, "Language").

usefulness, we were saying, would speech be in a country where the most essential words had lost their meaning in current usage?" (King, "Language," p. 228). Very few people can tolerate living in a state of paradox, and Vercors clearly perceived this dilemma and understood that a clandestine publishing house was precisely what was needed "to still the hunger of print-starved writers." Even in defeat and humiliation, then, it was the responsibility of intellectuals to speak out in order to preserve their very ethos. According to Vercors, "The point really was to show world opinion that France, amid misfortune and violence, was able to keep faith with the highest purpose: her claim to think straight" (Vercors, *Battle*, p. 155). In the land of Descartes, the act of epitomizing thought or, decidedly, of epiphanizing it, comes as no surprise. King so aptly emphasizes this propensity among French intellectuals: "The phrase 'sauvegarde de la pensée' is a significant one. We know that in the earliest stages of the occupation, many writers conceived their role to be that of guardians, curators of the cultural heritage" (King, "Language," p. 232). This being so, intellectuals would have a special responsibility: "the role of intellectuals would be similar in short to that of monks who, during the long night of the Middle Ages, had obstinately and secretly passed on the flame of ancient thought, keeping it lit for nearly a thousand years until the Renaissance." (King, "Language," p. 232). Vercors, too, in his comments on the novel in the definitive edition of *Le Silence de la mer*, views the flowering of clandestine literature as a spiritual movement, ". . . a moment in the history of the spirit and more precisely in French thought,"[5] and he affirms that his novella is an aspiration toward the spiritual purity of mankind.

Now, amid all this noble rhetoric, another paradox emerges, this one more disturbing than the first. King is the only critic who goes to the heart of the dilemma. He observes:

> The French have always attributed an excessive importance to literature and language. In all French intellectuals there is a subconscious belief that French culture is synonymous with universal culture. The myth of the power of words is similarly deep–seated, sustained by a hagiography including such figures as Voltaire, Hugo, Zola, and Péguy. It comes as no surprise to find the writers referred to above feeling that by retreating into language they were simultaneously serving their country's cause. In

5. Vercors, *Le Silence de la mer* (Paris, 1964), p. 131 (hereafter cited in the text as Vercors, *Silence*, with pagination according to the reprint in this volume).

a way scarcely imaginable in another country, many French writers could, without feelings of guilt, pursue their literary and intellectual activities. Cultural values are identified, or confused, with national and political values. (King, "Language," p. 237)

King goes on to cite an incisive slogan by Louis Martin–Chauffier that supports this notion: "My country, the French language, is not imperialist, it is apostolic" (King, "Language," p. 237). These remarks on the synonymy of French culture with universal culture and the protection, as it were, or preservation of this way of thinking undermine the very values they are supposed to safeguard. Hence the paradox remains, as King sees only too clearly:

> Even if it is legitimate to see various forms of literature as integral parts of resistance to barbarism and tyranny, is it not also true that to remain attached to literary and intellectual values at a time when news was filtering through of the concentration camps shows a degree of disingenuousness, even of insensitivity? Surely, if European civilization had culminated in the death–camps, it is perverse to respect the traditional values of this civilization, and, more so, to attempt to perpetuate them. (King, "Language," p. 238)

Vercors and his fellow resistance writers were well aware of this problem, and he subsequently took up the question in other writings that followed *Le Silence de la mer* in which he focused upon the "gigantic lie about the nature of man." He has endeavored ever since to plumb the meaning of being in order to understand the nature of man.

Up until now, we have examined the extratextual aspects of the theme of silence, that is the role silence played during the early stages of the Occupation, its historical significance, and how eventually, through the efforts of Vercors and his compatriots, it became eroded, thus giving birth to an astoundingly eloquent discourse: *Le Silence de la mer*. From the historical point of view, silence was a weapon, an arm of resistance: it had a concrete, though paradoxically immaterial, utility. It was an act of refusal and disdain. But from another perspective, from an aesthetic and ontological optic, silence is ground zero, the void from which the word, the Logos, surges forth. It is that state of emptiness from which the text itself is generated. We have come to that crossroads where history and literature intersect and can now cast a different glance, one a bit askew perhaps, upon the process by which a text is organically engendered and shaped.

The process of forming, patterning, and shaping is essentially one of creating order out of disorder, or content out of emptiness. The act of writing naturally presupposes a kind of relationship to the world and its events, a potential tale to be told. In the case of Vercors, as we know, historical events played a large role in this development. We remember the circumstances of the Occupation that, according to Vercors, gave birth to this novella: his fascination with the theme of silence as he worked on the engravings of Poe's tales, his reading of Jünger's *Gardens and Streets* and his subsequent modeling of von Ebrennac on the cultured German, the officer in his mother's home with whom he never spoke, the conversation overheard in a café among a group of German officers discussing their strategy for denuding France of her spirit, and, of course, how the title came to him in a flash of metaphorical insight.

In addition to Vercors's own account of these facts, critics such as Konrad Bieber and Pierre Brodin have amply discussed the genesis of *Le Silence de la mer* in terms of both its content and style. But however insightful they may be, their critical observations remain anecdotal in themselves; they never really examine the intratextual and organic functions of the narrative. Bieber, for instance, evokes the double thesis of the novel: on the one hand, the attempt to evoke the dignity of refusal and, on the other, to demonstrate that even the best of Germans is, in the end, incapable of revolting against injustice.[6] Brodin, too, offers little more than a summary account of Vercors's novella: "*Le Silence de la mer* is a short narrative, in lines that are nearly classical. Useless details are carefully omitted. One can hardly guess the place of the action: somewhere, in France, near the sea, probably in the southwest."[7] Yet, within the following remarks are contained the central points of omission and semiosis, the making of a coherent world of signs: "The young woman obviously symbolizes France, but the art of the narrator is such that one never has the impression of dealing with an abstraction. This woman who utters only one word is evoked, more than by her words, by her silences, and by her gestures" (Brodin, *Présences* 1:325).

At this point, we would like to shift our focus to the poetics of *Le*

6. Konrad Bieber, *L'Allemagne*, p. 128.
7. Pierre Brodin, *Présences contemporaines* 1: p. 324 (hereafter cited in the text as Brodin, *Présences*).

Silence de la mer in order to examine the structure of its discourse and, hence, to return to the questions that we asked in the opening pages, namely: How does silence function? What is its capacity to signify? From the very outset, throughout the entire novel, and especially in its closing pages, the narrator reveals a self-conscious awareness of the creative potential of silence in the telling of his tale. Contradictory though it may seem, he purposely creates a silent environment around the characters in which communication occurs, not only between them but also with the reader. The story opens with a depiction of the events surrounding the arrival of the German officer at the narrator's home. Neither the narrator nor his niece utters a word; we hear only the narrative voice, a textual construct, but no dialogue between the officer and his French hosts ensues. Rather, the reader's attention is directed toward other communicative modes, notably sound, sight, and gesture:

> Nous entendîmes marcher, le bruit des talons sur le carreau. Ma nièce me regarda et posa sa tasse. Je regardai la mienne dans mes mains.
>
> Je vis l'immense silhouette, la casquette plate, l'imperméable jeté sur les épaules comme une cape.
>
> Ma nièce avait ouvert la porte et restait silencieuse.
>
> L'Officier, à la porte, dit: "S'il vous plaît." Sa tête fit un petit salut. Il sembla mesurer le silence.
>
> (Vercors, *Silence*, p. 42; Eng. trans., p. 72)

These brief passages serve as a microcosm for the narrative techniques used throughout the text: the ubiquitous emphasis on the self-imposed, stoic silence of the French vis-à-vis the enemy, the accentuation of sights and sounds other than voice to communicate perceptions, and the importance of gesture and body language in transmitting meanings beyond words.

Thus *Le Silence de la mer* contains both a politics of silence (silence as resistance, as scorn, as defeat, and so forth) and a poetics of silence according to which it is used to point to and activate other narrative codes. Vercors chose this narrative technique purposely:

> For the technique, I kept to the objective narration which, following Conrad's lead, I had adopted as a strict rule. I did not allow myself the licence under any circumstances of conveying a character's thought and

feelings by an introspective description, but only – as in real life – by what an outsider can see or hear: people's gestures, their hands which betray them, their words always full of ambiguity, the silences which lay their hearts bare without their suspecting it. (Vercors, *Battle*, pp. 151–52)

In other words, Vercors was portraying a muffled world of signs, a semiotic space in which thoughts, feelings, and values are conveyed but not articulated. And in the world of French letters, the choice of so simple and denuded a discourse bespeaks an eternal aesthetic value of the French: the pristine purity of *le style classique* with its eloquent economy and anecdotal simplicity.

Less purposeful perhaps, but quite apparent nonetheless throughout *Le Silence de la mer*, is the style of the visual artist in the construction of the narrative. Vercors was by trade an engraver; consequently, he attributes an unusual importance to visual space, lines, angles, vignettes, and tableaux in his descriptions.[8] The characters, for instance, are often depicted in a statuesque mode: "Il ne la regardait pas comme un homme regarde une femme, mais comme il regarde une statue" (Vercors, *Silence*, p. 47; Eng. trans., p. 76). On another occasion, the narrator describes von Ebrennac in similar fashion: "Je considérai le long buste devant l'instrument, la nuque penchée, les mains longues, fines, nerveuses" (Vercors, *Silence*, p. 51; Eng. trans., p. 81). Similarly, the niece is often viewed in profile: "Ses yeux s'attardaient sur le profil incliné de ma nièce" (Vercors, *Silence*, p. 45; Eng. trans., p. 75) and "Il regardait ma nièce, le pur profil têtu et fermé" (Vercors, *Silence*, p. 50; Eng. trans., p. 80). This technique is most often used to portray the young woman's stoic defiance of the occupier and her implacable will not to speak. Thus, the theme of silence itself is placed in the foreground at the textual level by the narrator's constant recourse to visual signs, for art, as the reader well knows, is a silent medium, a spatial phenomenon that imposes a certain distance between the observer and the observed. This distance is sustained within the story by the narrator and his niece vis-à-vis the German occupier, who is himself encroaching upon a space that does not belong to him; and it is maintained between the reader and the text as well

---

8. Konrad Bieber's remarks are insightful in this regard: "Les recherches techniques ne sont cependant pas la préoccupation principale de cet écrivain dont la puissance se manifeste surtout dans le dessin rectiligne, aux contours fortement marqués, plutôt que dans la nuance ciselée et raffinée." (*L'Allemagne*, p. 133).

since no explanations, motives, thoughts, or intentions are ever revealed to him. Both the German and the reader must decode the numerous and often ambiguous signs that are either visually displayed to them or else internally sensed.

Apart from the vignettes, the etched profiles, and the statuesque postures, narrative technique in *Le Silence de la mer* relies heavily on references and allusions to body language, with eyes, hands, facial expressions, and gestures being the most prominent. In the absence of speech, listening becomes extremely important: "Nous entendîmes marcher le bruit des talons sur le carreau" (Vercors, *Silence* p. 42; Eng. trans., p. 72). At the beginning of the story, when von Ebrennac comes to live on the narrator's estate, we hear the steps of the intruder, steps that are, metaphorically, those of the German armies marching through France. And subsequently, we hear rather than see the officer's movements about the house: we detect his pensiveness or agitation according to his pacing in the room above the salon; we sense the ambiguity of his character, at once loyal to his homeland and enamoured of French culture, in his uneven gait: one strong step, one weak step. "Nous entendîmes naître, et cette fois sans conteste, approcher, le battement irrégulier des pas familiers" (Vercors, *Silence*, p. 59; Eng. trans., p. 89).

Given the overall importance of the sense of sight in a silent world, the face and eyes become very significant. It is noteworthy that von Ebrennac's gaze is almost always direct. His eyes are at once the forceful eyes of the intruder and the conciliatory ones of the francophile, the eyes of a military man performing his duty and those of a sensitive musician. The narrator's eyes, on the other hand, are those of the pure observer who watches both his niece and von Ebrennac. It is through the narrator's eyes that we see events unfold. Finally, unlike von Ebrennac, the niece casts oblique looks, indirect glances, downward gazes and often looks away or avoids eye contact with him altogether. This is the look of defiance or scorn of the enemy. It is especially apparent in the early pages of the novel: "Ma nièce avait fermé la porte et restait adossée au mur, regardant droit devant elle" (Vercors, *Silence*, p. 42; Eng. trans., p. 72). And as the officer beholds her in her defiant immobility, we see her attitude reflected in her body position: "Ses yeux se posérent sur ma nièce, toujours raide et droite, et je pus regarder moi-même à loisir le profil puissant, le nez prominent et mince" (Vercors, *Silence*, p. 43; Eng. trans., p. 73). The narrator, in a moment of respite from the silent confrontation between the occupier and the occupied, suggests to his niece that they break this silence as a gesture of common humanity. The impact of her refusal is conveyed by her look and gestures: "Ma nièce leva son visage. Elle haussait très haut les sourcils, sur des yeux brillants et indignés. Je me sentis presque un peu rougir" (Vercors, *Silence*, p. 48; Eng. trans., p. 77).

As the story progresses, the niece's affection for von Ebrennac grows, but it is only in the final moments upon learning that he shall be departing forever that she offers him her eyes and voice simultaneously, perhaps the most eloquent possible avowal of her love:

> Il ne bougea pas. Il restait tout à fait immobile, et dans son visage immobile et tendu, les yeux étaient plus encore immobiles et tendus, attachés aux yeux – trop ouverts, trop pâles – de ma nièce. Cela dura, dura – combien de temps? – dura jusqu'à ce qu'enfin, la jeune fille remuât les lèvres. Les yeux de Werner brillèrent.
> J'entendis:
> – Adieu.
> (Vercors, *Silence*, p. 68; Eng. trans., p. 96–97).

Amid all of the kinesic codes of the novella, it is gesture or, more precisely, hand movements that are the most revealing nonverbal signs used by the narrator. Words may lie and looks may be diverted, but hands always tell the true story of the emotions. During his stay in the narrator's home, von Ebrennac pays nightly visits to his silent hosts and speaks of the marvels of French culture and of his hopes for a unified Europe after the war. In the first part of the novella, before she falls in love with von Ebrennac, the niece's attention is seemingly focused only on her knitting, a gesture of her refusal to converse (i.e., collaborate) and a symbol of the emotions and events that will be woven together as the story progresses. About midway through the narrative it becomes apparent to the reader that von Ebrennac and the niece are attracted to each other. During one of his monologues on the unification of France and Germany, he alludes to the fable of *The Beauty and the Beast* as a metaphor of the Occupation and the eventual reconciliation of France and Germany. And the Beauty (France, the narrator's niece) "sent moins la patte pesante, moins les chaînes de sa prison" (Vercors, *Silence*, p. 50; Eng. trans., p. 80–81). The heavy hand of the oppressor is lifted and the Beauty can now in her own right extend her hand in love to the Beast: "Elle cesse de haïr, elle tend la main" (Vercors, *Silence*, p. 50; Eng. trans., p. 81).

Hands are present everywhere in *Le Silence de la mer* and the characters are cognizant of their significance and symbolism. Indeed, the only activities of the niece that are described are knitting and making coffee. And it is no coincidence that the German officer is a pianist by profession, a consummate artist with agile and delicate hands, not the symbolically stolid stumps of the oppressor. As the love plot unfolds, hands and faces become ever more expressive. Imprisoned in a self-imposed silence, the niece's forced reticence is belied by the tensions in her hands: "Et moi je sentais l'âme de ma nièce s'agiter dans cette prison qu'elle avait elle-même construite, je le voyais à bien des signes dont le moindre était un léger tremblement des doigts" (Vercors, *Silence*, p. 53; Eng. trans., p. 83). On another occasion, when von Ebrennac talks about an adolescent romance, the niece's hands again show her agitation: "Il attendit, pour continuer, que ma nièce eût enfilé de nouveau le fil, qu'elle venait de casser" (Vercors, *Silence*, p. 54; Eng. trans., p. 84). And these gentle and dexterous hands of the weaver are symbolically contrasted with the violent, vulgar hands of von Ebrennac's girlfriend. Having been stung by a mosquito on a walk in the forest, the young lady unveils the cruel side of her character: "Puis je lui vis faire un geste vif de la main. 'J'en ai attrapé un, Werner! Oh! regardez, je vais le punir. Je lui – arrache – les pattes – l'une – après – l'autre . . .' et elle le faisait" (Vercors, *Silence*, p. 54; Eng. trans., p. 84). Cruelty is subsequently rendered metaphorical by von Ebrennac in his account of Hitler's intentions: "Et, vraiment, je sais bien que mes amis et notre Führer ont les plus grandes et les plus nobles idées. Mais je sais aussi qu'ils arracheraient aux moustiques les pattes l'une après l'autre" (Vercors, *Silence*, p. 54; Eng. trans., p. 84–85). The metaphor is then raised to the level of the universal in Werner's reference to some telling lines from *Macbeth*: "Maintenant il sent ses crimes secrets coller à ses mains" (Vercors, *Silence*, p. 56; Eng. trans., p. 86). These are the bloody, culpable hands of the tyrant; hands no longer capable of performing good works but only the heinous acts of a criminal.

By far the most demonstrative use of hand symbolism as a means of story telling occurs in the final pages of the novel when von Ebrennac returns to the home of the narrator, his dreams of unification having been shattered by some German officers who revealed their plans to mislead the French in order to destroy them. The intensity of Werner's inner turmoil betrays itself in his hands:

J'appris ce jour-là qu'une main peut, pour qui sait l'observer, refléter les émotions aussi bien qu'un visage, – aussi bien et mieux qu'un visage car elle échappe davantage au contrôle de la volonté. Et les doigts de cette main–là se tendaient et se pliaient, se pressaient et s'accrochaient, se livraient à la plus intense mimique tandis que le visage et tout le corps demeuraient immobiles et compassés. (Vercors, *Silence*, p. 61–62; Eng. trans., p. 91).

Humbling himself before the niece, von Ebrennac explains the dupery to which he fell victim. Her sense of deception and forlornness is also conveyed by her gestures: "La jeune fille lentement laissa tomber ses mains au creux de sa jupe, où elles demeurèrent penchées et inertes comme des barques échouées sur le sable" (Vercors, *Silence*, p. 62; Eng. trans., p. 91). In this paroxysm of emotion, as Werner tells the niece that he must bid her farewell and carry out his duty, it is the face and eyes that communicate the innermost feelings of the characters: "Et lentement elle leva la tête, et alors, pour la première fois, – pour la première fois – elle offrit à l'officier le regard de ses yeux pâles" (Vercors, *Silence*, p. 62; Eng. trans., p. 91). His profound anger and despair may be read on his face and in his eyes: "Il serrait les mâchoires avec une telle énergie que je voyais saillir les pommettes, et une veine épaisse et tortueuse comme un ver, battre sous la tempe. . . . Et ses yeux s'accrochèrent aux yeux pâles et dilatés de ma nièce" (Vercors, *Silence*, p. 63–64; Eng. trans., p. 92–93). Von Ebrennac, this best of all possible Germans as Vercors called him, ultimately submits to the will of a tyrant, his act of submission signalled by his gestures: "Puis il laissa retomber sa main," and "Il se redressa, et son visage et tout son corps semblèrent s'assoupir comme après un bain reposant" (Vercors, *Silence*, p. 69; Eng. trans., p. 97).

Casting a retrospective glance upon *Le Silence de la mer*, we come to realize that apart from the monologues von Ebrennac delivers to his French hosts by the fireside, the narrator and his niece speak only once each. It is astounding that so much information can be transmitted by the other sensory and kinesic codes we have examined. What is all the more amazing is the fact that silence is made to function not only at the diegetic level of the text but also at the metaphorical and metonymical levels as well. Space does not allow us to analyze these imagistic functions of silence; however, it would be appropriate to point them out to the reader. We have already seen the technique of portraying the statuesque body, the fixed eyes, and the "hard look," but images of plasticity, immobility, and hardness are also used to convey attitudes and conditions. The Occupation itself is a "hard reality" symbolized by the heavy burden that the occupying troops represent, by military apparel such as Werner's helmet, and by armored vehicles. Along with the images of hardness come the weight of oppressiveness and of silence. Among other phenomena, the narrator alludes to heavy gasses, "comme un gaz pesant et irrespirable" (Vercors, *Silence*, p. 53; Eng. trans., p. 83), to the burden that silence imposes, "L'immobilité de ma nièce, la mienne aussi sans doute, alourdissaient ce silence" (Vercors, *Silence*, p. 43; Eng. trans., p. 73), and to stolid objects such as walls. One feels both the weight of the oppressor's presence and the weight of the oppressed's refusal to comply. Metonymically, this motif also manifests itself in the architectural descriptions. There are numerous references to walls and enclosures that we may label the prison motif, since the French are in effect prisoners in their own homes. To go outdoors is to face the enemy, to acknowledge his presence. Hence, by extension, weather conditions are portrayed as menacing, rain and snow being the only ones described by the narrator. The characters, even Werner, are drawn to the fire, the hearth, a symbol of conviviality and the homeland – the very soul of France: "Mais cette pièce a une âme. Toute cette maison a une âme" (Vercors, *Silence*, p. 49; Eng. trans., p. 78).

Other imagistic systems in *Le Silence de la mer* are given a semantic charge as well. We have seen that intertextual references to the theme of silence occurred to the author when he was working on the engravings for Poe's "Silence," and the narrator alludes to the central image that had come to Vercors during the genesis of the novella: "Certes, sous les silences d'antan, – comme, sous la calme surface des eaux, la mêlée des bêtes dans la mer, – je sentais bien grouiller la vie sous-marine des sentiments cachés, des désirs et des pensées qui se nient et qui luttent" (Vercors, *Silence*, p. 65; Eng. trans., p. 94). We have also seen that fable and allegory play a role in the telling of the story, especially *The Beauty and the Beast*. These imagistic codes generally serve to point out oppositions between France and Germany. They are carefully interwoven with other images in the text that underscore French delicacy as opposed to Germanic ponderousness. Thus, the landscape of France is made to echo her finesse: "Chez moi c'est bien dur. Très. Les arbres sont des sapins, des forêts serrées, la neige est lourde là-dessus. Ici les arbres sont fins. La neige dessus c'est une dentelle. Chez moi on pense à un taureau, trapu et puissant, qui a besoin de sa force pour vivre. Ici c'est l'esprit, la pensée subtile et poétique" (Vercors, *Silence*, p. 46; Eng. trans., p. 75).

The most effective imagery of all in depicting the French temperament as opposed to the German temperament is that based on literature and music. Literature, the most sublime use of language, is, for von Ebrennac, the epitome of *francité*: "Les Anglais, reprit-il, on pense aussitôt: Shakespeare. Les Italiens: Dante. L'Espagne: Cervantes. Et nous, tout de suite: Goethe. Après, il faut chercher. Mais si on dit: et la France? Alors, qui surgit à l'instant? Molière? Racine? Hugo? Voltaire? Rabelais? ou quel autre?" (Vercors, *Silence*, p. 49; Eng. trans., p. 79). On the other hand, it is in music that the spirit of Germany resides: "Mais pour la musique, alors c'est chez nous: Bach, Haendel, Beethoven, Wagner, Mozart . . . quel nom vient le premier?" (Vercors, *Silence*, p. 49; Eng. trans., p. 79). As von Ebrennac explores this metaphor more closely, he reduces it to the creations on one emblematic figure, Bach, whose music he finds otherwordly: "Cela nous fait comprendre, non: deviner . . . non : pressentir . . . pressentir ce qu'est la nature . . . la nature divine et inconnaissable . . . la nature . . . désinvestie . . . de l'âme humaine. Oui: c'est une musique inhumaine" (Vercors, *Silence*, p. 51; Eng. trans., p. 81). Thus, the very soul of Germany is its nonhuman quality, its fundamental character of *dépassement*. Is von Ebrennac thereby saying that the soul that produced this music is the same soul that produced Hitler? Are we tottering between nonhumanity and inhumanity? Perhaps so, because Werner's deepest desire is to produce music on a human scale: "Je veux faire, moi, une musique à la mesure de l'homme" (Vercors, *Silence*, p. 52; Eng. trans., p. 82); and to accomplish this he needs the acquiescence of France:

> Maintenant j'ai besoin de la France. Mais je demande beaucoup: je demande qu'elle m'accueille . . . Sa richesse, sa haute richesse, on ne peut la conquérir. Il faut la boire à son sein, il faut qu'elle vous offre son sein dans un mouvement et un sentiment maternels . . . Il faut qu'elle accepte de comprendre notre soif, qu'elle accepte de l'étancher . . . qu'elle accepte de s'unir à nous. (Vercors, *Silence*, p. 52; Eng. trans., p. 82)

This theme of unification, as we have seen in the fable of *The Beauty and the Beast*, is the leitmotif of von Ebrennac's monologues. It grows out of his sincere desire that France and Germany will be united for the benefit of all and it echoes his hidden desire to marry the narrator's niece eventually – a wish never to be fulfilled.

In this introduction we have endeavored to examine the theme of silence in both its extratextual and textual dimensions as well as its intratextual function of generating other narrative codes and signifying devices. In doing so, we have run the risk of overstating the novella's eloquent discourse, of making silence speak more loquaciously than Vercors had intended. For, ultimately, the dialogue must take place in the words and interstices between the reader and the author. In the final analysis, it is best to allow *Le Silence de la mer* to speak for itself. That we shall do in the pages that follow.

Le Silence de la mer

Il fut précédé par un grand déploiement d'appareil militaire. D'abord deux troufions,[1] tous deux très blonds, l'un dégingandé[2] et maigre, l'autre carré, aux mains de carrier.[3] Ils regardèrent la maison, sans entrer. Plus tard vint un sous officier. Le troufion dégingandé l'accompagnait. Ils me parlèrent, dans ce qu'ils supposaient être du français. Je ne comprenais pas un mot. Pourtant je leur montrai les chambres libres. Ils parurent contents.

Le lendemain matin, un torpédo militaire,[4] gris et énorme, pénétra dans le jardin. Le chauffeur et un jeune soldat mince, blond et souriant, en extirpèrent deux caisses, et un gros ballot[5] entouré de toile grise. Ils montèrent le tout dans la chambre la plus vaste. Le torpédo repartit, et quelques heures plus tard j'entendis une cavalcade. Trois cavaliers apparurent. L'un d'eux mit pied à terre et s'en fut visiter[6] le vieux bâtiment de pierre. Il revint, et tous, hommes et chevaux, entrèrent dans la grange qui me sert d'atelier. Je vis plus tard qu'ils avaient enfoncé le valet de mon établi entre deux pierres, dans un trou du mur, attaché une corde au valet, et les chevaux à la corde.

Pendant deux jours il ne se passa plus rien. Je ne vis plus personne. Les cavaliers sortaient de bonne heure avec leurs chevaux, ils les ramenaient le soir, et eux-mêmes couchaient dans la paille[7] dont ils avaient garni la soupente.[8]

Puis, le lendemain du troisième jour, le grand torpédo revint. Le jeune homme souriant chargea une cantine spacieuse sur son épaule et la porta dans la chambre. Il prit ensuite son sac qu'il déposa dans

---

1. *deux troufions*: two soldiers; privates (slang)
2. *dégingandé*: gangly; lanky
3. *aux mains de carrier*: with hands like those of a quarry worker
4. *un torpédo militaire*: an open truck; jeep
5. *un gros ballot*: a large bundle; package
6. *s'en fut visiter*: went out to visit
7. *la paille*: straw
8. *la soupente*: stall

la chambre voisine. Il descendit et, s'adressant à ma nièce dans un français correct, demanda des draps.

Ce fut ma nièce qui alla ouvrir quand on frappa. Elle venait de me servir mon café, comme chaque soir (le café me fait dormir). J'étais assis au fond de la pièce, relativement dans l'ombre. La porte donne sur le jardin, de plain-pied. Tout le long de la maison court un trottoir de carreaux[9] rouges très commode quand il pleut. Nous entendîmes marcher, le bruit des talons sur le carreau. Ma nièce me regarda et posa sa tasse. Je gardai la mienne dans mes mains.

Il faisait nuit, pas très froid: ce novembre-là ne fut pas très froid. Je vis l'immense silhouette, la casquette plate, l'imperméable jeté sur les épaules comme une cape.

Ma nièce avait ouvert la porte et restait silencieuse. Elle avait rabattu la porte sur le mur, elle se tenait elle-même contre le mur, sans rien regarder. Moi je buvais mon café, à petits coups.

L'officier, à la porte, dit: «S'il vous plaît.» Sa tête fit un petit salut. Il sembla mesurer le silence. Puis il entra.

La cape glissa[10] sur son avant-bras, il salua militairement et se découvrit.[11] Il se tourna vers ma nièce, sourit discrètement en inclinant très légèrement le buste. Puis il me fit face et m'adressa une révérence plus grave. Il dit: «Je me nomme Werner von Ebrennac.» J'eus le temps de penser, très vite: «Le nom n'est pas allemand. Descendant d'émigré protestant?» Il ajouta: «Je suis désolé.»

Le dernier mot, prononcé en traînant, tomba dans le silence. Ma nièce avait fermé la porte et restait adossée au mur,[12] regardant droit devant elle. Je ne m'étais pas levé. Je déposai lentement ma tasse vide sur l'harmonium et croisai mes mains et attendis.

L'officier reprit: «Cela était naturellement nécessaire. J'eusse évité si cela était possible. Je pense mon ordonnance fera tout pour votre tranquillité.» Il était debout au milieu de la pièce. Il était immense et très mince. En levant le bras il eût touché les solives.[13]

Sa tête était légèrement penchée en avant, comme si le cou n'eût pas été planté sur les épaules, mais à la naissance de la poitrine. Il

9. *carreaux*: tiles
10. *glissa*: slid
11. *se découvrit*: took off his hat
12. *adossée au mur*: (her) back against the wall
13. *les solives*: joists; beams

n'était pas voûté mais cela faisait comme s'il l'était. Ses hanches[14] et ses épaules étroites étaient impressionnantes. Le visage était beau. Viril et marqué de deux grandes dépressions le long des joues. On ne voyait pas les yeux, que cachait l'ombre portée de l'arcade. Ils me parurent clairs. Les cheveux étaient blonds et souples jetés en arrière, brillant soyeusement[15] sous la lumière du lustre.

Le silence se prolongeait. Il devenait de plus en plus épais, comme le brouillard du matin. Épais et immobile. L'immobilité de ma nièce, la mienne aussi sans doute, alourdissaient[16] ce silence, le rendaient de plomb. L'officier lui-même, désorienté, restait immobile, jusqu'à ce qu'enfin je visse naître un sourire sur ses lèvres. Son sourire était grave et sans nulle trace d'ironie. Il ébaucha un geste[17] de la main, dont la signification m'échappa. Ses yeux se posèrent sur ma nièce, toujours raide et droite, et je pus regarder moi-même à loisir le profil puissant, le nez proéminent et mince. Je voyais, entre les lèvres mijointes, briller une dent d'or. Il détourna enfin les yeux et regarda le feu dans la cheminée et dit: «J'éprouve un grand estime pour les personnes qui aiment leur patrie», et il leva brusquement la tête et fixa l'ange sculpté au-dessus de la fenêtre. «Je pourrais maintenant monter à ma chambre, dit-il. Mais je ne connais pas le chemin.» Ma nièce ouvrit la porte qui donne sur le petit escalier et commença de gravir[18] les marches, sans un regard pour l'officier, comme si elle eût été seule. L'officier la suivit. Je vis alors qu'il avait une jambe raide.

Je les entendis traverser l'antichambre, les pas de l'Allemand résonnèrent dans le couloir, alternativement forts et faibles, une porte s'ouvrit, puis se referma. Ma nièce revint. Elle reprit sa tasse et continua de boire son café. J'allumai une pipe. Nous restâmes silencieux quelques minutes. Je dis: «Dieu merci, il a l'air convenable.» Ma nièce haussa les épaules. Elle attira sur ses genoux ma veste de velours et termina la pièce invisible qu'elle avait commencé d'y coudre.

14. *ses hanches*: hips
15. *brillant soyeusement*: with a silky shine
16. *alourdissaient*: weighed upon
17. *il ébaucha un geste*: he made a slight gesture
18. *gravir*: to climb

Le lendemain matin l'officier descendit quand nous prenions notre petit déjeuner dans la cuisine. Un autre escalier y mène et je ne sais si l'Allemand nous avait entendus ou si ce fut par hasard qu'il prit ce chemin. Il s'arrêta sur le seuil et dit: «J'ai passé une très bonne nuit. Je voudrais que la vôtre était aussi bonne.» Il regardait la vaste pièce en souriant. Comme nous avions peu de bois et encore moins de charbon, je l'avais repeinte, nous y avions amené quelques meubles, des cuivres et des assiettes anciennes, afin d'y confiner notre vie pendant l'hiver. Il examinait cela et l'on voyait luire le bord de ses dents très blanches. Je vis que ses yeux n'étaient pas bleus comme je l'avais cru, mais dorés. Enfin, il traversa la pièce et ouvrit la porte sur le jardin. Il fit deux pas et se retourna pour regarder notre longue maison basse, couverte de treilles,[19] aux vieilles tuiles[20] brunes. Son sourire s'ouvrit largement.

«Votre vieux maire m'avait dit que je logerais au château, dit-il en désignant d'un revers de main[21] la prétentieuse bâtisse[22] que les arbres dénudés[23] laissaient apercevoir, un peu plus haut sur le coteau.[24] Je féliciterai mes hommes qu'ils se sont trompés. Ici c'est un beaucoup plus beau château.»

Puis il referma la porte, nous salua à travers les vitres, et partit.

Il revint le soir à la même heure que la veille. Nous prenions notre café. Il frappa mais n'attendit pas que ma nièce lui ouvrît. Il ouvrit lui-même: «Je crains que je vous dérange, dit-il. Si vous le préférez, je passerai par la cuisine: alors vous fermerez cette porte à clef.» Il traversa la pièce, et resta un moment la main sur la poignée, regardant les divers coins du fumoir. Enfin il eut une petite inclinaison du buste: «Je vous souhaite une bonne nuit», et il sortit.

Nous ne fermâmes jamais la porte à clef. Je ne suis pas sûr que les raisons de cette abstention fussent très claires ni très pures. D'un accord tacite nous avions décidé, ma nièce et moi, de ne rien changer à notre vie, fût-ce le moindre détail: comme si l'officier n'existait pas; comme s'il eût été un fantôme. Mais il se peut qu'un autre sentiment se mêlât dans mon cœur à cette volonté: je ne puis sans souffrir offenser un homme, fût-il mon ennemi.

Pendant longtemps, – plus d'un mois, – la même scène se répéta

---

19. *treilles*: arbors
20. *tuiles*: tiles
21. *d'un revers de main*: with the back of his hand
22. *bâtisse*: building
23. *dénudés*: bare
24. *le coteau*: slope; hill

chaque jour. L'officier frappait et entrait. Il prononçait quelques mots sur le temps, la température, ou quelque autre sujet de même importance: leur commune propriété étant qu'ils ne supposaient pas de réponse. Il s'attardait toujours un peu au seuil de la petite porte. Il regardait autour de lui. Un très léger sourire traduisait le plaisir qu'il semblait prendre à cet examen, – le même examen chaque jour et le même plaisir. Ses yeux s'attardaient sur le profil incliné de ma nièce, immanquablement[25] sévère et insensible, et quand enfin il détournait son regard j'étais sûr d'y pouvoir lire une sorte d'approbation[26] souriante. Puis il disait en s'inclinant: «Je vous souhaite une bonne nuit», et il sortait.

Les choses changèrent brusquement un soir. Il tombait au dehors une neige fine mêlée de pluie, terriblement glaciale et mouillante. Je faisais brûler dans l'âtre[27] des bûches épaisses que je conservais pour ces jours-là. Malgré moi j'imaginais l'officier, dehors, l'aspect saupoudré[28] qu'il aurait en entrant. Mais il ne vint pas. L'heure était largement passée de sa venue et je m'agaçais[29] de reconnaître qu'il occupait ma pensée. Ma nièce tricotait lentement, d'un air très appliqué.

Enfin des pas se firent entendre. Mais ils venaient de l'intérieur de la maison. Je reconnus, à leur bruit inégal, la démarche de l'officier. Je compris qu'il était entré par l'autre porte, qu'il venait de sa chambre. Sans doute n'avait-il pas voulu paraître à nos yeux sous un uniforme trempé et sans prestige: il s'était d'abord changé.

Les pas, – un fort, un faible, – descendirent l'escalier. La porte s'ouvrit et l'officier parut. Il était en civil. Le pantalon était d'épaisse flanelle grise, la veste de tweed bleu acier enchevêtré de mailles d'un brun chaud.[30] Elle était large et ample, et tombait avec un négligé plein d'élégance. Sous la veste, un chandail de grosse laine écrue[31] moulait[32] le torse mince et musclé.

«Pardonnez-moi, dit-il. Je n'ai pas chaud. J'étais très mouillé et ma chambre est très froide. Je me chaufferai quelques minutes à votre feu.»

25. *immanquablement*: without fail
26. *approbation*: approval
27. *l'âtre*: fireplace; hearth
28. *saupoudré*: sprinkled (with powder)
29. *je m'agaçais*: I was troubled
30. *enchevêtré de mailles d'un brun chaud*: mixed with a warm brown knit
31. *écrue*: natural colored
32. *moulait*: hugged; fit tightly

Il s'accroupit[33] avec difficulté devant l'âtre, tendit les mains. Il les tournait et les retournait. Il disait: «Bien! . . . Bien! . . .» Il pivota et présenta son dos à la flamme, toujours accroupi et tenant un genou dans ses bras.

«Ce n'est rien ici, dit-il. L'hiver en France est une douce saison. Chez moi c'est bien dur. Très. Les arbres sont des sapins, des forêts serrées, la neige est lourde là-dessus. Ici les arbres sont fins. La neige dessus c'est une dentelle.[34] Chez moi on pense à un taureau, trapu[35] et puissant, qui a besoin de sa force pour vivre. Ici c'est l'esprit, la pensée subtile et poétique.»

Sa voix était assez sourde, très peu timbrée. L'accent était léger, marqué seulement sur les consonnes dures. L'ensemble ressemblait à un bourdonnement[36] plutôt chantant.

Il se leva. Il appuya l'avant-bras sur le linteau[37] de la haute cheminée, et son front sur le dos de sa main. Il était si grand qu'il devait se courber un peu, moi je ne me cognerais[38] pas même le sommet de la tête.

Il demeura sans bouger assez longtemps, sans bouger et sans parler. Ma nièce tricotait avec une vivacité mécanique. Elle ne jeta pas les yeux sur lui, pas une fois. Moi je fumais, à demi allongé dans mon grand fauteuil douillet.[39] Je pensais que la pesanteur de notre silence ne pourrait pas être secouée.[40] Que l'homme allait nous saluer et partir.

Mais le bourdonnement sourd et chantant s'éleva de nouveau, on ne peut dire qu'il rompit[41] le silence, ce fut plutôt comme s'il en était né.

«J'aimai toujours la France, dit l'officier sans bouger. Toujours. J'étais un enfant à l'autre guerre et ce que je pensais alors ne compte pas. Mais depuis je l'aimai toujours. Seulement c'était de loin. Comme la Princesse Lointaine.» Il fit une pause avant de dire gravement: «A cause de mon père.»

Il se retourna et, les mains dans les poches de sa veste, s'appuya le

33. *il s'accroupit*: he bent over
34. *une dentelle*: a lace
35. *trapu*: stocky
36. *un bourdonnement*: a drone; a humming
37. *le linteau*: lintel
38. *je ne me cognerais*: I wouldn't even bump
39. *douillet*: soft
40. *secouée*: shaken off
41. *rompit*: broke

long du jambage.[42] Sa tête cognait un peu sur la console. De temps en temps il s'y frottait lentement l'occipital,[43] d'un mouvement naturel de cerf. Un fauteuil était là offert, tout près. Il ne s'y assit pas. Jusqu'au dernier jour, il ne s'assit jamais. Nous ne le lui offrîmes pas et il ne fit rien, jamais, qui pût passer pour de la familiarité.

Il répéta:

«A cause de mon père. Il était un grand patriote. La défaite a été une violente douleur. Pourtant il aima la France. Il aima Briand, il croyait dans la République de Weimar et dans Briand. Il était très enthousiaste. Il disait: «Il va nous unir, comme mari et femme.» Il pensait que le soleil allait enfin se lever sur l'Europe . . .»

En parlant il regardait ma nièce. Il ne la regardait pas comme un homme regarde une femme, mais comme il regarde une statue. Et en fait, c'était bien une statue. Une statue animée, mais une statue.

«. . . Mais Briand fut vaincu. Mon père vit que la France était encore menée par vos Grands Bourgeois cruels, – les gens comme vos de Wendel, vos Henri Bordeaux et votre vieux Maréchal. Il me dit: «Tu ne devras jamais aller en France avant d'y pouvoir entrer botté et casqué.»[44] Je dus le promettre, car il était près de la mort. Au moment de la guerre, je connaissais toute l'Europe, sauf la France.»

Il sourit et dit, comme si cela avait été une explication:

«Je suis musicien.»

Une bûche s'effondra, des braises[45] roulèrent hors du foyer. L'Allemand se pencha, ramassa les braises avec des pincettes.[46] Il poursuivit:

«Je ne suis pas exécutant: je compose de la musique. Cela est toute ma vie, et, ainsi, c'est une drôle de figure pour moi de me voir en homme de guerre. Pourtant je ne regrette pas cette guerre. Non. Je crois que de ceci il sortira de grandes choses . . .»

Il se redressa,[47] sortit ses mains des poches et les tint à demi levées:

«Pardonnez-moi: peut-être j'ai pu vous blesser. Mais ce que je disais, je le pense avec un très bon cœur: je le pense par amour pour

---

42. *jambage*: door jamb
43. *l'occipital*: cheekbone
44. *botté et casqué*: in boots and a helmet
45. *braises*: sparks; cinders
46. *pincettes*: tongs
47. *il se redressa*: he stood erect

la France. Il sortira de très grandes choses pour l'Allemagne et pour la France. Je pense, après mon père, que le soleil va luire sur l'Europe.»

Il fit deux pas et inclina le buste. Comme chaque soir il dit: «Je vous souhaite une bonne nuit.» Puis il sortit.

Je terminai silencieusement ma pipe. Je toussai un peu et je dis: «C'est peut-être inhumain de lui refuser l'obole[48] d'un seul mot.» Ma nièce leva son visage. Elle haussait très haut les sourcils, sur des yeux brillants et indignés. Je me sentis presque un peu rougir.

Depuis ce jour, ce fut le nouveau mode de ses visites. Nous ne le vîmes plus que rarement en tenue.[49] Il se changeait d'abord et frappait ensuite à notre porte. Etait-ce pour nous épargner la vue de l'uniforme ennemi? Ou pour nous le faire oublier, – pour nous habituer à sa personne? Les deux, sans doute. Il frappait, et entrait sans attendre une réponse qu'il savait que nous ne donnerions pas. Il le faisait avec le plus candide naturel, et venait se chauffer au feu, qui était le prétexte constant de sa venue, – un prétexte dont ni lui ni nous n'étions dupes, dont il ne cherchait pas même à cacher le caractère commodément conventionnel.

Il ne venait pas absolument chaque soir, mais je ne me souviens pas d'un seul où il nous quittât sans avoir parlé. Il se penchait sur le feu et, tandis qu'il offrait à la chaleur de la flamme quelque partie de lui-même, sa voix bourdonnante s'élevait doucement, et ce fut au long de ces soirées, sur les sujets qui habitaient son cœur, – son pays, la musique, la France, – un interminable monologue; car pas une fois il ne tenta d'obtenir de nous une réponse, un acquiescement, ou même un regard. Il ne parlait pas longtemps, – jamais beaucoup plus longtemps que le premier soir. Il prononçait quelques phrases, parfois brisées de silences, parfois s'enchaînant avec la continuité monotone d'une prière. Quelquefois immobile contre la cheminée, comme une cariatide, quelquefois s'approchant, sans s'interrompre, d'un objet, d'un dessin au mur. Puis il se taisait, il s'inclinait et nous souhaitait une bonne nuit.

Il dit une fois (c'était dans les premiers temps de ses visites): «Où est la différence entre un feu de chez moi et celui-ci? Bien sûr le bois, la flamme, la cheminée se ressemblent. Mais non la lumière.

48. *l'obole*: offering
49. *en tenue*: in uniform

Celle-ci dépend des objets qu'elle éclaire, – des habitants de ce fumoir, des meubles, des murs, des livres sur les rayons . . .

«Pourquoi aimé-je tant cette pièce? dit-il pensivement. Elle n'est pas si belle, – pardonnez-moi! . . .» Il rit: «Je veux dire: ce n'est pas une pièce de musée . . . Vos meubles, on ne dit pas: voilà des merveilles . . . Non . . . Mais cette pièce a une âme. Toute cette maison a une âme.»

Il était devant les rayons de la bibliothèque. Ses doigts suivaient les reliures[50] d'une caresse légère.

« . . . Balzac, Barrès, Baudelaire, Beaumarchais, Boileau, Buffon . . . Chateaubriand, Corneille, Descartes, Fénelon, Flaubert . . . La Fontaine, France, Gautier, Hugo . . . Quel appel!» dit-il avec un rire léger et hochant la tête. «Et je n'en suis qu'à la lettre H! . . . Ni Molière, ni Rabelais, ni Racine, ni Pascal, ni Stendhal, ni Voltaire, ni Montaigne, ni tous les autres! . . .» Il continuait de glisser lentement le long des livres, et de temps en temps il laissait échapper un imperceptible «Ha!», quand, je suppose, il lisait un nom auquel il ne songeait pas. «Les Anglais, reprit-il, on pense aussitôt: Shakespeare. Les Italiens: Dante. L'Espagne: Cervantès. Et nous, tout de suite: Gœthe. Après, il faut chercher. Mais si on dit: et la France? Alors, qui surgit à l'instant? Molière? Racine? Hugo? Voltaire? Rabelais? ou quel autre? Ils se pressent, ils sont comme une foule à l'entrée d'un théâtre, on ne sait pas qui faire entrer d'abord.»

Il se retourna et dit gravement:

«Mais pour la musique, alors c'est chez nous: Bach, Haendel, Beethoven, Wagner, Mozart . . . quel nom vient le premier?

«Et nous nous sommes fait la guerre!» dit-il lentement en remuant la tête. Il revint à la cheminée et ses yeux souriants se posèrent sur le profil de ma nièce. «Mais c'est la dernière! Nous ne nous battrons plus: nous nous marierons!» Ses paupières se plissèrent, les dépressions sous les pommettes[51] se marquèrent de deux longues fossettes,[52] les dents blanches apparurent. Il dit gaiement: «Oui, oui!» Un petit hochement de tête répéta l'affirmation. «Quand nous sommes entrés à Saintes, poursuivit-il après un silence, j'étais heureux que la population nous recevait bien. J'étais très heureux. Je pensais: Ce sera facile. Et puis, j'ai vu que ce n'était

---

50. *les reliures*: bindings (of a book)
51. *les pommettes*: cheekbones
52. *des fossettes*: dimples

pas cela du tout, que c'était la lâcheté.»[53] Il était devenu grave. «J'ai méprisé ces gens. Et j'ai craint pour la France. Je pensais: Est-elle *vraiment* devenue ainsi?» Il secoua la tête: «Non! Non. Je l'ai vu ensuite; et maintenant, je suis heureux de son visage sévère.»

Son regard se porta sur le mien – que je détournai, – il s'attarda un peu en divers points de la pièce, puis retourna sur le visage, impitoyablement insensible, qu'il avait quitté.

«Je suis heureux d'avoir trouvé ici un vieil homme digne. Et une demoiselle silencieuse. Il faudra vaincre ce silence. Il faudra vaincre le silence de la France. Cela me plaît.»

Il regardait ma nièce, le pur profil têtu[54] et fermé, en silence et avec une insistance grave, où flottaient encore pourtant les restes d'un sourire. Ma nièce le sentait. Je la voyais légèrement rougir, un pli peu à peu s'inscrire entre ses sourcils. Ses doigts tiraient un peu trop vivement, trop sèchement sur l'aiguille, au risque de rompre le fil.

«Oui, reprit la lente voix bourdonnante, c'est mieux ainsi. Beaucoup mieux. Cela fait des unions solides, – des unions où chacun gagne de la grandeur . . . Il y a un très joli conte pour les enfants, que j'ai lu, que vous avez lu, que tout le monde a lu. Je ne sais si le titre est le même dans les deux pays. Chez moi il s'appelle: *Das Tier und die Schöne*, – la Belle et la Bête. Pauvre Belle! La Bête la tient à merci, – impuissante et prisonnière, – elle lui impose à toute heure du jour son implacable et pesante présence . . . La Belle est fière, digne, – elle s'est faite dure . . . Mais la Bête vaut mieux qu'elle ne semble. Oh, elle n'est pas très dégrossie![55] Elle est maladroite, brutale, elle paraît bien rustre auprès de la Belle si fine! . . . Mais elle a du cœur, oui, elle a une âme qui aspire à s'élever. Si la Belle voulait! . . . La Belle met longtemps à vouloir. Pourtant, peu à peu, elle découvre au fond des yeux du geôlier haï[56] une lueur, – un reflet où peuvent se lire la prière et l'amour. Elle sent moins la patte pesante,[57] moins les chaînes de sa prison . . . Elle cesse de haïr, cette constance la touche, elle tend la main . . . Aussitôt la Bête se transforme, le sortilège[58] qui la maintenait dans ce pelage[59] barbare

53. *la lâcheté*: cowardice
54. *têtu*: stubborn
55. *dégrossie*: polished
56. *(un) geôlier haï*: hated jailer
57. *la patte pesante*: heavy paw
58. *le sortilège*: spell
59. *ce pelage*: this fur

est dissipé: c'est maintenant un chevalier très beau et très pur, délicat et cultivé, que chaque baiser de la Belle pare[60] de qualités toujours plus rayonnantes . . . Leur union détermine un bonheur sublime. Leurs enfants, qui additionnent et mêlent les dons de leurs parents, sont les plus beaux que la terre ait portés . . .

«N'aimiez-vous pas ce conte? Moi je l'aimai toujours. Je le relisais sans cesse. Il me faisait pleurer. J'aimais surtout la Bête, parce que je comprenais sa peine. Encore aujourd'hui, je suis ému quand j'en parle.»

Il se tut, respira avec force, et s'inclina:

«Je vous souhaite une bonne nuit.»

Un soir, – j'étais monté dans ma chambre pour y chercher du tabac, – j'entendis s'élever le chant de l'harmonium. On jouait ces «VIIIᵉ Prélude et Fugue» que travaillait ma nièce avant la débâcle. Le cahier était resté ouvert à cette page mais, jusqu'à ce soir-là, ma nièce ne s'était pas résolue à de nouveaux exercices. Qu'elle les eût repris souleva en moi du plaisir et de l'étonnement: quelle nécessité intérieure pouvait bien l'avoir soudain décidée?

Ce n'était pas elle. Elle n'avait pas quitté son fauteuil ni son ouvrage. Son regard vint à la rencontre du mien, m'envoya un message que je ne déchiffrai pas.[61] Je considérai le long buste devant l'instrument, la nuque penchée, les mains longues, fines, nerveuses, dont les doigts se déplaçaient sur les touches comme des individus autonomes.

Il joua seulement le Prélude. Il se leva, rejoignit le feu.

«Rien n'est plus grand que cela», dit-il de sa voix sourde qui ne s'éleva pas beaucoup plus haut qu'un murmure. «Grand? . . . ce n'est pas même le mot. Hors de l'homme, – hors de sa chair.[62] Cela nous fait comprendre, non: deviner . . . non: pressentir . . .[63] pressentir ce qu'est la nature . . . la nature divine et inconnaissable . . . la nature . . . désinvestie . . .[64] de l'âme humaine. Oui: c'est une musique inhumaine.»

Il parut, dans un silence songeur, explorer sa propre pensée. Il se

60. *pare*: adorns
61. *je ne déchiffrai pas*: (that) I didn't decipher
62. *sa chair*: his flesh
63. *pressentir*: sense
64. *désinvestie*: divested

mordillait[65] lentement une lèvre.

«Bach . . . Il ne pouvait être qu'Allemand. Notre terre a ce caractère: ce caractère inhumain. Je veux dire: pas à la mesure de l'homme.»

Un silence, puis:

«Cette musique-là, je l'aime, je l'admire, elle me comble, elle est en moi comme la présence de Dieu mais . . . Mais ce n'est pas la mienne.

«Je veux faire, moi, une musique à la mesure de l'homme: cela aussi est un chemin pour atteindre la vérité. C'est *mon* chemin. Je n'en voudrais, je n'en pourrais suivre un autre. Cela, maintenant, je le sais. Je le sais tout à fait. Depuis quand? Depuis que je vis ici.»

Il nous tourna le dos. Il appuya ses mains au linteau, s'y retint par les doigts et offrit son visage à la flamme entre ses avant-bras, comme à travers les barreaux d'une grille. Sa voix se fit plus sourde et plus bourdonnante:[66]

«Maintenant j'ai besoin de la France. Mais je demande beaucoup: je demande qu'elle m'accueille. Ce n'est rien, être chez elle comme un étranger, – un voyageur ou un conquérant. Elle ne donne rien alors, – car on ne peut rien lui prendre. Sa richesse, sa haute richesse, on ne peut la conquérir. Il faut la boire à son sein, il faut qu'elle vous offre son sein dans un mouvement et un sentiment maternels . . . Je sais bien que cela dépend de nous . . . Mais cela dépend d'elle aussi. Il faut qu'elle accepte de comprendre notre soif, et qu'elle accepte de l'étancher . . . qu'elle accepte de s'unir à nous.»

Il se redressa,[67] sans cesser de nous tourner le dos, les doigts toujours accrochés à la pierre.

«Moi, dit-il un peu plus haut, il faudra que je vive ici, longtemps. Dans une maison pareille à celle-ci. Comme le fils d'un village pareil à ce village . . . Il faudra . . .»

Il se tut. Il se tourna vers nous. Sa bouche souriait, mais non ses yeux qui regardaient ma nièce.

«Les obstacles seront surmontés, dit-il. La sincérité toujours surmonte les obstacles.

«Je vous souhaite une bonne nuit.»

---

65. *il se mordillait*: he was biting
66. *bourdonnante*: droning
67. *il se redressa*: he straightened up

Je ne puis me rappeler, aujourd'hui, tout ce qui fut dit au cours de plus de cent soirées d'hiver. Mais le thème n'en variait guère. C'était la longue rapsodie de sa découverte de la France: l'amour qu'il en avait de loin, avant de la connaître, et l'amour grandissant chaque jour qu'il éprouvait depuis qu'il avait le bonheur d'y vivre. Et, ma foi, je l'admirais. Oui: qu'il ne se décourageât pas. Et que jamais il ne fût tenté de secouer cet implacable silence par quelque violence de langage . . . Au contraire, quand parfois il laissait ce silence envahir la pièce et la saturer jusqu'au fond des angles comme un gaz pesant et irrespirable, il semblait bien être celui de nous trois qui s'y trouvait le plus à l'aise. Alors il regardait ma nièce, avec cette expression d'approbation à la fois souriante et grave qui avait été la sienne dès le premier jour. Et moi je sentais l'âme de ma nièce s'agiter dans cette prison qu'elle avait elle-même construite, je le voyais à bien des signes dont le moindre était un léger tremblement des doigts. Et quand enfin Werner von Ebrennac dissipait ce silence, doucement et sans heurt par le filtre de sa bourdonnante voix, il semblait qu'il me permît de respirer plus librement.

Il parlait de lui, souvent:

«Ma maison dans la forêt, j'y suis né, j'allais à l'école du village, de l'autre côté; je ne l'ai jamais quittée, jusqu'à ce que j'étais à Munich, pour les examens, et à Salzbourg, pour la musique. Depuis, j'ai toujours vécu là-bas. Je n'aimais pas les grandes villes. J'ai connu Londres, Vienne, Rome, Varsovie, les villes allemandes naturellement. Je n'aime pas pour vivre. J'aimais seulement beaucoup Prague, – aucune autre ville n'a autant d'âme. Et surtout Nuremberg. Pour un Allemand, c'est la ville qui dilate son cœur, parce qu'il retrouve là les fantômes chers à son cœur, le souvenir dans chaque pierre de ceux qui firent la noblesse de la vieille Allemagne. Je crois que les Français doivent éprouver la même chose, devant la cathédrale de Chartres. Ils doivent aussi sentir tout contre eux la présence des ancêtres, – la grâce de leur âme, la grandeur de leur foi, et leur gentillesse. Le destin m'a conduit sur Chartres. Oh vraiment, quand elle apparaît, par-dessus les blés mûrs, toute bleue de lointain et transparente, immatérielle, c'est une grande émotion! J'imaginais les sentiments de ceux qui venaient jadis[68] à elle, à pied, à cheval ou sur des chariots . . . Je partageais ces sentiments et j'aimais ces gens, et comme je voudrais être leur frère!»

68. *jadis*: in former times

Son visage s'assombrit:[69]

«Cela est dur à entendre sans doute d'un homme qui venait sur Chartres dans une grande voiture blindée . . .[70] Mais pourtant c'est vrai. Tant de choses remuent ensemble dans l'âme d'un Allemand, même le meilleur! Et dont il aimerait tant qu'on le guérisse . . .» Il sourit de nouveau, un très léger sourire qui graduellement éclaira tout le visage, puis:

«Il y a dans le château voisin de chez nous une jeune fille . . . Elle est très belle et très douce. Mon père toujours se réjouissait[71] si je l'épouserais. Quand il est mort nous étions presque fiancés, on nous permettait de faire de grandes promenades, tous les deux seuls.»

Il attendit, pour continuer, que ma nièce eût enfilé de nouveau le fil, qu'elle venait de casser. Elle le faisait avec une grande application, mais le chas[72] était très petit et ce fut difficile. Enfin elle y parvint.

«Un jour, reprit-il, nous étions dans la forêt. Les lapins, les écureuils filaient[73] devant nous. Il y avait toutes sortes de fleurs, – des jonquilles,[74] des jacinthes sauvages,[75] des amaryllis . . . La jeune fille s'exclamait de joie. Elle dit: «Je suis heureuse, Werner. J'aime, oh! j'aime ces présents de Dieu!» J'étais heureux, moi aussi. Nous nous allongeâmes sur la mousse,[76] au milieu des fougères.[77] Nous ne parlions pas. Nous regardions au-dessus de nous les cimes des sapins[78] se balancer, les oiseaux voler de branche en branche. La jeune fille poussa un petit cri: «Oh! il m'a piquée sur le menton! Sale petite bête, vilain petit moustique!»[79] Puis je lui vis faire un geste vif de la main. «J'en ai attrapé un, Werner! Oh! regardez, je vais le punir: je lui – arrache – les pattes[80] – l'une – après – l'autre . . .» et elle le faisait . . .

«Heureusement, continua-t-il, elle avait beaucoup d'autres

69. *s'assombrit*: grew dark
70. *voiture blindée*: armored car
71. *se réjouissait*: would be delighted
72. *le chas*: eye (of a knitting needle)
73. *les écureuils filaient*: squirrels were running about
74. *des jonquilles*: daffodils
75. *des jacinthes sauvages*: wild hyacinths
76. *sur la mousse*: on the moss
77. *des fougères*: ferns
78. *les cimes des sapins*: tops of the pines
79. *moustique*: mosquito
80. *arracher les pattes*: tear off (its) legs

prétendants.[81] Je n'eus pas de remords. Mais aussi j'étais effrayé pour toujours à l'égard des jeunes filles allemandes.»

Il regarda pensivement l'intérieur de ses mains et dit:

«Ainsi sont aussi chez nous les hommes politiques. C'est pourquoi je n'ai jamais voulu m'unir à eux, malgré mes camarades qui m'écrivaient: «Venez nous rejoindre.» Non: je préférai rester toujours dans ma maison. Ce n'était pas bon pour le succès de la musique, mais tant pis: le succès est peu de chose, auprès d'une conscience en repos. Et, vraiment, je sais bien que mes amis et notre Führer ont les plus grandes et les plus nobles idées. Mais je sais aussi qu'ils arracheraient aux moustiques les pattes l'une après l'autre. C'est cela qui arrive aux Allemands toujours quand ils sont très seuls: cela remonte toujours. Et qui de plus «seuls» que les hommes du même Parti, quand ils sont les maîtres?

«Heureusement maintenant ils ne sont plus seuls: ils sont en France. La France les guérira. Et je vais vous dire: ils le savent. Ils savent que la France leur apprendra à être des hommes vraiment grands et purs.»

Il se dirigea vers la porte. Il dit d'une voix retenue,[82] comme pour lui-même:

«Mais pour cela il faut l'amour.»

Il tint un moment la porte ouverte; le visage tourné sur l'épaule, il regardait la nuque de ma nièce penchée sur son ouvrage, la nuque frêle et pâle d'où les cheveux s'élevaient en torsades[83] de sombre acajou. Il ajouta, sur un ton de calme résolution:

«Un amour partagé.»

Puis il détourna la tête, et la porte se ferma sur lui tandis qu'il prononçait d'une voix rapide les mots quotidiens:

«Je vous souhaite une bonne nuit.»

Les longs jours printaniers arrivaient. L'officier descendait maintenant aux derniers rayons du soleil. Il portait toujours son pantalon de flanelle grise, mais sur le buste une veste plus légère en jersey de laine couleur de bure[84] couvrait une chemise de lin[85] au col ouvert. Il descendit un soir, tenant un livre refermé sur l'index. Son visage s'éclairait de ce demi-sourire contenu, qui préfigure le plaisir

---

81. *prétendants*: suitors
82. *d'une voix retenue*:: in a restrained voice
83. *en torsades*: coiled
84. *couleur de bure*: the color of a monk's frock
85. *chemise de lin*: a linen shirt

escompté[86] d'autrui. Il dit:

«J'ai descendu ceci pour vous. C'est une page de *Macbeth*. Dieux! Quelle grandeur!»

Il ouvrit le livre:

«C'est la fin. La puissance de Macbeth file entre ses doigts, avec l'attachement de ceux qui mesurent enfin la noirceur de son ambition. Les nobles seigneurs qui défendent l'honneur de l'Écosse attendent sa ruine prochaine. L'un d'eux décrit les symptômes dramatiques de cet écroulement . . .»[87]

Et il lut lentement, avec une pesanteur pathétique:

ANGUS

Maintenant il sent ses crimes secrets coller[88] à ses mains. A chaque minute, des hommes de cœur révoltés lui reprochent sa mauvaise foi. Ceux qu'il commande obéissent à la crainte et non plus à l'amour. Désormais il voit son titre pendre autour de lui, flottant comme la robe d'un géant sur le nain[89] qui l'a volée.

Il releva la tête et rit. Je me demandais avec stupeur s'il pensait au même tyran que moi. Mais il dit:

«N'est-ce pas là ce qui doit troubler les nuits de votre Amiral? Je plains[90] cet homme, vraiment, malgré le mépris qu'il m'inspire comme à vous. *Ceux qu'il commande obéissent à la crainte et non plus à l'amour.* Un chef qui n'a pas l'amour des siens est un bien misérable mannequin. Seulement . . . seulement . . . pouvait-on souhaiter autre chose? Qui donc, sinon un aussi morne[91] ambitieux, eût accepté ce rôle? Or il le fallait. Oui, il fallait quelqu'un qui acceptât de vendre sa patrie parce que, aujourd'hui, – aujourd'hui et pour longtemps, la France ne peut tomber volontairement dans nos bras ouverts sans perdre à ses yeux sa propre dignité. Souvent la plus sordide entremetteuse[92] est ainsi à la base de la plus heureuse alliance. L'entremetteuse n'en est pas moins méprisable, ni l'alliance moins heureuse.»

Il fit claquer le livre en le fermant, l'enfonça dans la poche de sa

---

86. *escompté*: anticipated
87. *écroulement*: downfall
88. *coller*: stick to
89. *le nain*: dwarf
90. *je plains*: I pity
91. *morne*: dejected
92. *l'entremetteuse*: procuress

veste et d'un mouvement machinal frappa deux fois cette poche de la paume de la main. Puis son long visage éclairé d'une expression heureuse, il dit:

«Je dois prévenir mes hôtes que je serai absent pour deux semaines. Je me réjouis[93] d'aller à Paris. C'est maintenant le tour de ma permission et je la passerai à Paris, pour la première fois. C'est un grand jour pour moi. C'est le plus grand jour, en attendant un autre que j'espère avec toute mon âme et qui sera encore un plus grand jour. Je saurai l'attendre des années, s'il le faut. Mon cœur a beaucoup de patience.

«A Paris, je suppose que je verrai mes amis, dont beaucoup sont présents aux négociations que nous menons avec vos hommes politiques, pour préparer la merveilleuse union de nos deux peuples. Ainsi je serai un peu le témoin de ce mariage . . . Je veux vous dire que je me réjouis pour la France, dont les blessures de cette façon cicatriseront[94] très vite, mais je me réjouis bien plus encore pour l'Allemagne et pour moi-même! Jamais personne n'aura profité de sa bonne action, autant que fera l'Allemagne en rendant sa grandeur à la France et sa liberté!

«Je vous souhaite une bonne nuit.»

---

93. *je me réjouis*: I am delighted
94. *cicatriseront*: will heal

Othello

Éteignous cette lumière,
pour ensuite éteindre
celle de la vie

Nous ne le vîmes pas quand il revint.

Nous le savions là, parce que la présence d'un hôte dans une maison se révèle par bien des signes, même lorsqu'il reste invisible. Mais pendant de nombreux jours, – beaucoup plus d'une semaine, – nous ne le vîmes pas.

L'avouerai-je? Cette absence ne me laissait pas l'esprit en repos. Je pensais à lui, je ne sais pas jusqu'à quel point je n'éprouvais pas du regret, de l'inquiétude. Ni ma nièce ni moi nous n'en parlâmes. Mais lorsque parfois le soir nous entendions là-haut résonner sourdement[95] les pas inégaux, je voyais bien, à l'application têtue[96] qu'elle mettait soudain à son ouvrage, à quelques lignes légères qui marquaient son visage d'une expression à la fois butée[97] et attentive, qu'elle non plus n'était pas exempte de pensées pareilles aux miennes.

Un jour je dus aller à la Kommandantur,[98] pour une quelconque déclaration de pneus. Tandis que je remplissais le formulaire[99] qu'on m'avait tendu, Werner von Ebrennac sortit de son bureau. Il ne me vit pas tout d'abord. Il parlait au sergent, assis à une petite table devant un haut miroir au mur. J'entendais sa voix sourde aux inflexions chantantes et je restais là, bien que je n'eusse plus rien à y faire, sans savoir pourquoi, curieusement ému, attendant je ne sais quel dénouement.[100] Je voyais son visage dans la glace, il me paraissait pâle et tiré.[101] Ses yeux se levèrent, ils tombèrent sur les miens, pendant deux secondes nous nous regardâmes, et brusquement il pivota sur ses talons et me fit face. Ses lèvres s'entrouvrirent et avec lenteur il leva légèrement une main, que presque aussitôt il laissa retomber. Il secoua imperceptiblement la tête avec une

95. *sourdement*: with a dull sound
96. *têtue*: stubborn
97. *butée*: determined
98. *la Kommandantur*: headquarters [German]
99. *le formulaire*: form
100. *dénouement*: outcome
101. *tiré*: drawn

irrésolution pathétique, comme s'il se fût dit: non, à lui-même, sans pourtant me quitter des yeux. Puis il esquissa[102] une inclination du buste en laissant glisser son regard à terre, et il regagna, en clochant,[103] son bureau, où il s'enferma.

De cela je ne dis rien à ma nièce. Mais les femmes ont une divination de félin.[104] Tout au long de la soirée elle ne cessa de lever les yeux de son ouvrage, à chaque minute, pour les porter sur moi; pour tenter de lire quelque chose sur un visage que je m'efforçais de tenir impassible,[105] tirant sur ma pipe avec application. A la fin, elle laissa tomber ses mains, comme fatiguée, et, pliant l'étoffe,[106] me demanda la permission de s'aller coucher de bonne heure. Elle passait deux doigts lentement sur son front comme pour chasser une migraine. Elle m'embrassa et il me sembla lire dans ses beaux yeux gris un reproche et une assez pesante tristesse. Après son départ je me sentis soulevé par une absurde colère: la colère d'être absurde et d'avoir une nièce absurde. Qu'est-ce que c'était que toute cette idiotie? Mais je ne pouvais pas me répondre. Si c'était une idiotie, elle semblait bien enracinée.[107]

Ce fut trois jours plus tard que, à peine avions-nous vidé nos tasses, nous entendîmes naître, et cette fois sans conteste approcher, le battement irrégulier des pas familiers. Je me rappelai brusquement ce premier soir d'hiver où ces pas s'étaient fait entendre, six mois plus tôt. Je pensai: «Aujourd'hui aussi il pleut.» Il pleuvait durement depuis le matin. Une pluie régulière et entêtée,[108] qui noyait tout à l'entour et baignait l'intérieur même de la maison d'une atmosphère froide et moite.[109] Ma nièce avait couvert ses épaules d'un carré de soie imprimé où dix mains inquiétantes, dessinées par Jean Cocteau, se désignaient mutuellement avec mollesse;[110] moi je réchauffais mes doigts sur le fourneau de ma pipe, – et nous étions en juillet!

Les pas traversèrent l'antichambre et commencèrent de faire gémir les marches.[111] L'homme descendait lentement, avec une

---

102. *esquissa*: made a slight inclination
103. *en clochant*: hobbling
104. *une divination de félin*: catlike instinct
105. *impassible*: unmoved
106. *l'étoffe*: material; fabric
107. *enracinée*: rooted
108. *entêtée*: stubborn; persistent
109. *moite*: moist
110. *mollesse*: limpness
111. *faire gémir les marches*: to make the stairs moan

lenteur sans cesse croissante, mais non pas comme un qui hésite: comme un dont la volonté subit une exténuante épreuve.[112] Ma nièce avait levé la tête et elle me regardait, elle attacha sur moi, pendant tout ce temps, un regard transparent et inhumain de grand-duc. Et quand la dernière marche eut crié et qu'un long silence suivit, le regard de ma nièce s'envola,[113] je vis les paupières s'alourdir,[114] la tête s'incliner et tout le corps se confier au dossier[115] du fauteuil avec lassitude.

Je ne crois pas que ce silence ait dépassé quelques secondes. Mais ce furent de longues secondes. Il me semblait voir l'homme, derrière la porte, l'index levé prêt à frapper, et retardant, retardant le moment où, par le seul geste de frapper il allait engager l'avenir . . . Enfin il frappa. Et ce ne fut ni avec la légèreté de l'hésitation, ni la brusquerie de la timidité vaincue, ce furent trois coups pleins et lents, les coups assurés et calmes d'une décision sans retour. Je m'attendais à voir comme autrefois la porte aussitôt s'ouvrir. Mais elle resta close, et alors je fus envahi par une incoercible agitation d'esprit, où se mêlait à l'interrogation l'incertitude des désirs contraires, et que chacune des secondes qui s'écoulaient,[116] me semblait-il, avec une précipitation croissante de cataracte, ne faisait que rendre plus confuse et sans issue. Fallait-il répondre? Pourquoi ce changement? Pourquoi attendait-il que nous rompions[117] ce soir un silence dont il avait montré par son attitude antérieure combien il en approuvait la salutaire[118] ténacité? Quels étaient ce soir, – ce soir, – les commandements de la dignité?

Je regardai ma nièce, pour pêcher dans ses yeux un encouragement ou un signe. Mais je ne trouvai que son profil. Elle regardait le bouton de la porte. Elle le regardait avec cette fixité inhumaine de grand-duc qui m'avait déjà frappé, elle était très pâle et je vis, glissant sur les dents dont apparut une fine ligne blanche, se lever la lèvre supérieure dans une contraction douloureuse; et moi, devant ce drame intime soudain dévoilé[119] et qui dépassait de si haut le tourment bénin de mes tergiversations,[120] je perdis mes dernières

112. *épreuve*: test
113. *s'envola*: faded
114. *s'alourdir*: grow heavy
115. *se confier au dossier*: fall back into the armchair
116. *s'écoulaient*: passed
117. *nous rompions*: we break
118. *salutaire*: beneficial
119. *dévoilé*: unveiled
120. *tergiversations*: evasiveness

forces. A ce moment deux nouveaux coups furent frappés, – deux seulement, deux coups faibles et rapides, – et ma nièce dit: «Il va partir . . .» d'une voix basse et si complètement découragée que je n'attendis pas davantage et dis d'une voix claire: «Entrez, monsieur.»

Pourquoi ajoutai-je: monsieur? Pour marquer que j'invitais l'homme et non l'officier ennemi? Ou, au contraire, pour montrer que je n'ignorais pas *qui* avait frappé et que c'était bien à celui-là que je m'adressais? Je ne sais. Peu importe. Il subsiste que je dis: entrez, monsieur; et qu'il entra.

J'imaginais le voir paraître en civil et il était en uniforme. Je dirais volontiers qu'il était plus que jamais en uniforme, si l'on comprend par là qu'il m'apparut clairement que, cette tenue, il avait endossée[121] dans la ferme intention de nous en imposer la vue. Il avait rabattu la porte[122] sur le mur et il se tenait droit dans l'embrasure,[123] si droit et si raide que j'en étais presque à douter si j'avais devant moi le même homme et que, pour la première fois, je pris garde à sa ressemblance surprenante avec l'acteur Louis Jouvet. Il resta ainsi quelques secondes droit, raide et silencieux, les pieds légèrement écartés et les bras tombant sans expression le long du corps, et le visage si froid, si parfaitement impassible, qu'il ne semblait pas que le moindre sentiment pût l'habiter.

Mais moi qui étais assis dans mon fauteuil profond et avais le visage à hauteur de sa main gauche, je voyais cette main, mes yeux furent saisis par cette main et y demeurèrent comme enchaînés, à cause du spectacle pathétique qu'elle me donnait et qui démentait[124] pathétiquement toute l'attitude de l'homme . . .

J'appris ce jour-là qu'une main peut, pour qui sait l'observer, refléter les émotions aussi bien qu'un visage, – aussi bien et mieux qu'un visage car elle échappe davantage au contrôle de la volonté. Et les doigts de cette main-là se tendaient[125] et se pliaient, se

121. *endossée*: put on
122. *rabattu la porte*: opened
123. *l'embrasure*: doorway
124. *démentait*: was belying
125. *se tendaient*: opened
    se pliaient: closed
    se pressaient: squeezed
    s'accrochaient: clinched
    se livraient: gave themselves over to "And the fingers of that hand were opening and closing, squeezing and clinching, giving themselves over to the most intense mimicking, while the face and the whole body remained immobile and stiff."

pressaient et s'accrochaient, se livraient à la plus intense mimique tandis que le visage et tout le corps demeuraient immobiles et compassés.[126]

Puis les yeux parurent revivre, ils se portèrent un instant sur moi, – il me sembla être guetté par un faucon,[127] – des yeux luisants entre les paupières écartées et raides, les paupières à la fois fripées[128] et raides d'un être tenu par l'insomnie. Ensuite ils se posèrent sur ma nièce – et ils ne la quittèrent plus.

La main enfin s'immobilisa, tous les doigts repliés et crispés[129] dans la paume, la bouche s'ouvrit (les lèvres en se séparant firent: «Pp . . . » comme le goulot débouché[130] d'une bouteille vide), et l'officier dit, – sa voix était plus sourde que jamais:

«Je dois vous adresser des paroles graves.»

Ma nièce lui faisait face mais elle baissait la tête. Elle enroulait autour de ses doigts la laine d'une pelote,[131] tandis que la pelote se défaisait en roulant sur le tapis; ce travail absurde était le seul sans doute qui pût encore s'accorder à son attention abolie, – et lui épargner[132] la honte.

L'officier reprit, – l'effort était si visible qu'il semblait que ce fût au prix de sa vie:

«Tout ce que j'ai dit ces six mois, tout ce que les murs de cette pièce ont entendu . . . » – il respira, avec un effort d'asthmatique, garda un instant la poitrine gonflée . . .[133] «il faut . . . » Il respira: «il faut l'oublier».

Le jeune fille lentement laissa tomber ses mains au creux[134] de sa jupe, où elles demeurèrent penchées[135] et inertes comme des barques échouées sur le sable, et lentement elle leva la tête, et alors, pour la première fois, – pour la première fois – elle offrit à l'officier le regard de ses yeux pâles.

Il dit (à peine si je l'entendis): *Oh welch'ein Licht!*, pas même un

126. *compassés*: stiff
127. *guetté par un faucon*: eyed by a falcon
128. *fripées*: tired
129. *repliés et crispés*: coiled and tense
130. *le goulot débouché*: the open neck
131. *une pelote*: a ball (of thread)
132. *épargner*: to spare
133. *gonflée*: expanded
134. *au creux*: in the hollow
135. *penchées*: drooping
    échouées: stranded
". . . where they remained drooping and inert like boats stranded on the sand . . ."

murmure; et comme si en effet ses yeux n'eussent pas pu supporter cette lumière, il les cacha derrière son poignet.[136] Deux secondes; puis il laissa retomber sa main, mais il avait baissé les paupières et ce fut à lui désormais de tenir ses regards à terre.

Ses lèvres firent: «Pp . . .» et il prononça, – la voix était sourde, sourde, sourde:

«J'ai vu ces hommes victorieux.»

Puis, après quelques secondes, d'une voix plus basse encore:

«Je leur ai parlé.» Et enfin dans un murmure, avec une lenteur amère:

«Ils ont ri de moi.»

Il leva les yeux sur ma personne et avec gravité hocha[137] trois fois imperceptiblement la tête. Les yeux se fermèrent, puis:

«Ils ont dit: «Vous n'avez pas compris que nous les bernons?»[138] Ils ont dit cela. Exactement. *Wir prellen sie.* Ils ont dit: «Vous ne supposez pas que nous allons sottement laisser la France se relever à notre frontière? Non?» Ils rirent très fort. Ils me frappaient joyeusement le dos en regardant ma figure: «Nous ne sommes pas des musiciens!»

Sa voix marquait, en prononçant ces derniers mots, un obscur mépris, dont je ne sais s'il reflétait ses propres sentiments à l'égard des autres, ou le ton même des paroles de ceux-ci.

«Alors j'ai parlé longtemps, avec beaucoup de véhémence. Ils faisaient: «Tst! Tst!» Ils ont dit: «La politique n'est pas un rêve de poète. Pourquoi supposez-vous que nous avons fait la guerre? Pour leur vieux Maréchal?» Ils ont encore ri: «Nous ne sommes pas des fous ni des niais:[139] nous avons l'occasion de détruire la France, elle le sera. Pas seulement sa puissance: son âme aussi. Son âme surtout. Son âme est le plus grand danger. C'est notre travail en ce moment: ne vous y trompez pas, mon cher! Nous la pourrirons par nos sourires et nos ménagements. Nous en ferons une chienne rampante.»[140]

Il se tut. Il semblait essoufflé.[141] Il serrait les mâchoires avec une telle énergie que je voyais saillir les pommettes,[142] et une veine,

136. *son poignet*: his wrist
137. *hocha*: nodded
138. *nous les bernons*: we are making fools of them
139. *des niais*: simpletons
140. *une chienne rampante*: a crawling bitch
141. *essoufflé*: out of breath
142. *que je voyais saillir les pommettes*: that I saw his cheekbones stand out

épaisse et tortueuse comme un ver, battre sous la tempe. Soudain toute la peau de son visage remua, dans une sorte de frémissement souterrain,[143] – comme fait un coup de brise sur un lac; comme, aux premières bulles, la pellicule de crème durcie[144] à la surface d'un lait qu'on fait bouillir. Et ses yeux s'accrochèrent[145] aux yeux pâles et dilatés de ma nièce, et il dit, sur un ton bas, uniforme, intense et oppressé, avec une lenteur accablée:[146]

«Il n'y a pas d'espoir.» Et d'une voix plus sourde encore et plus basse, et plus lente, comme pour se torturer lui-même de cette intolérable constatation: «Pas d'espoir. Pas d'espoir.» Et soudain, d'une voix inopinément haute et forte, et à ma surprise claire et timbrée, comme un coup de clairon,[147] – comme un cri: «Pas d'espoir!»

Ensuite, le silence.

Je crus l'entendre rire. Son front, bourrelé et fripé,[148] ressemblait à un grelin d'amarre.[149] Ses lèvres tremblèrent, – des lèvres de malade à la fois fiévreuses et pâles.

«Ils m'ont blâmé, avec un peu de colère: «Vous voyez bien! Vous voyez combien vous l'aimez! Voilà le grand Péril! Mais nous guérirons l'Europe de cette peste! Nous la purgerons de ce poison!» Ils m'ont tout expliqué, oh! ils ne m'ont rien laissé ignorer. Ils flattent vos écrivains, mais en même temps, en Belgique, en Hollande, dans tous les pays qu'occupent nos troupes, ils font déjà le barrage.[150] Aucun livre français ne peut plus passer, – sauf les publications techniques, manuels de dioptrique[151] ou formulaires de cémentation . . .[152] Mais les ouvrages de culture générale, aucun. Rien!»

Son regard passa par-dessus ma tête, volant et se cognant[153] aux coins de la pièce comme un oiseau de nuit égaré. Enfin il sembla

---

"He clenched his jaws with such force that I saw his cheekbones stand out, and a vein, thick and serpentine like a worm, pulsate under his temple."

143. *frémissement souterrain*: underground shivering
144. *la pellicule de crème durcie*: film of hardened cream
145. *s'accrochèrent*: fixed upon
146. *accablée*: worn out
147. *timbrée comme un coup de clairon*: sonorous as the sound of a trumpet
148. *bourrelé et fripé*: tormented and tired
149. *un grelin d'amarre*: mooring rope
150. *ils font déjà le barrage*: they are already blocking off
151. *dioptrique*: refraction
152. *formulaires de cémentation*: instructions on case hardening (metallurgy)
153. *se cognant*: bumping against

trouver refuge sur les rayons les plus sombres, – ceux où s'alignent Racine, Ronsard, Rousseau. Ses yeux restèrent accrochés[154] là et sa voix reprit, avec une violence gémissante:[155]

«Rien, rien, personne!» Et comme si nous n'avions pas compris encore, pas mesuré l'énormité de la menace: «Pas seulement vos modernes! Pas seulement vos Péguy, vos Proust, vos Bergson . . . Mais tous les autres! Tous ceux-là! Tous! Tous!»

Son regard encore une fois balaya les reliures doucement luisant dans la pénombre,[156] comme pour une caresse désespérée.

«Ils éteindront la flamme tout à fait! cria-t-il. L'Europe ne sera plus éclairée par cette lumière!»

Et sa voix creuse[157] et grave fit vibrer jusqu'au fond de ma poitrine, inattendu et saisissant, le cri dont l'ultime syllabe traînait[158] comme une frémissante plainte:

«Nevermore!»

Le silence tomba une fois de plus. Une fois de plus mais, cette fois, combien plus obscur et tendu! Certes, sous les silences d'antan, – comme, sous la calme surface des eaux, la mêlée des bêtes dans la mer, – je sentais bien grouiller[159] la vie sous-marine des sentiments cachés, des désirs et des pensées qui se nient et qui luttent. Mais sous celui-ci, ah! rien qu'une affreuse oppression . . .

La voix brisa enfin ce silence. Elle était douce et malheureuse.

«J'avais un ami. C'était mon frère. Nous avions étudié de compagnie.[160] Nous habitions la même chambre à Stuttgart. Nous avions passé trois mois ensemble à Nuremberg. Nous ne faisions rien l'un sans l'autre: je jouais devant lui ma musique; il me lisait ses poèmes. Il était sensible et romantique. Mais il me quitta. Il alla lire ses poèmes à Munich, devant de nouveaux compagnons. C'est lui qui m'écrivait sans cesse de venir les retrouver. C'est lui que j'ai vu à Paris avec ses amis. J'ai vu ce qu'ils ont fait de lui!»

Il remua lentement la tête, comme s'il eût dû opposer un refus douloureux à quelque supplication.

«Il était le plus enragé! Il mélangeait la colère et le rire. Tantôt il

---

154. *accrochés*: fastened
155. *gémissante*: creaking
156. *balaya les reliures doucement luisant dans la pénombre*: swept over the bindings softly shining in the shadows
157. *creuse*: hollow
158. *traînait*: was drawn out
159. *grouiller*: swarming
160. *de compagnie*: together

me regardait avec flamme et criait: «C'est un venin![161] Il faut vider la bête de son venin!» Tantôt il donnait dans mon estomac des petits coups du bout de son index: «Ils ont la grande peur maintenant, ah, ah! ils craignent pour leurs poches et pour leur ventre, – pour leur industrie et leur commerce! Ils ne pensent qu'à ça! Les rares autres, nous les flattons et les endormons, ah, ah! . . . . Ce sera facile!» Il riait et sa figure devenait toute rose: «Nous échangerons leur âme contre un plat de lentilles!»[162]

Werner respira:

«J'ai dit: «Avez-vous mesuré ce que vous faites? L'avez-vous MESURÉ?» Il a dit: «Attendez-vous que cela nous intimide? Notre lucidité est d'une autre trempe!»[163] J'ai dit: «Alors vous scellerez[164] ce tombeau? – à jamais?» Il a dit: «C'est la vie ou la mort. Pour conquérir suffit la Force: pas pour dominer. Nous savons très bien qu'une armée n'est rien pour dominer. – Mais au prix de l'Esprit! criai-je. Pas à ce prix! – L'esprit ne meurt jamais, dit-il. Il en a vu d'autres. Il renaît de ses cendres. Nous devons bâtir pour dans mille ans: d'abord il faut détruire.» Je le regardais. Je regardais au fond de ses yeux clairs. Il était sincère, oui. C'est ça le plus terrible.»

Ses yeux s'ouvrirent très grands, – comme sur le spectacle de quelque abominable meurtre:[165]

«Ils feront ce qu'ils disent!» s'écria-t-il comme si nous n'avions pas dû le croire. «Avec méthode et persévérance! Je connais ces diables acharnés!»[166]

Il secoua la tête, comme un chien qui souffre d'une oreille. Un murmure passa entre ses dents serrées, le «oh!» gémissant et violent de l'amant trahi.

Il n'avait pas bougé. Il était toujours immobile, raide[167] et droit dans l'embrasure de la porte, les bras allongés comme s'ils eussent eu à porter des mains de plomb;[168] et pâle, – non pas comme de la cire,[169] mais comme le plâtre de certains murs délabrés: gris, avec des taches plus blanches de salpêtre.

161. *un venin*: venom
162. *lentilles*: lentils
163. *d'une autre trempe*: of another kind
164. *vous scellerez*: you will seal
165. *meurtre*: murder
166. *acharnés*: stubborn
167. *raide*: stiff
168. *plomb*: lead
169. *la cire*: wax
      le plâtre: plaster

Je le vis lentement incliner le buste. Il leva une main. Il la projeta, la paume en dessous, les doigts un peu pliés, vers ma nièce, vers moi. Il la contracta, il l'agita un peu tandis que l'expression de son visage se tendait avec une sorte d'énergie farouche.[170] Ses lèvres s'entrouvrirent, et je crus qu'il allait nous lancer je ne sais quelle exhortation: je crus, – oui, je crus qu'il allait nous encourager à la révolte. Mais pas un mot ne franchit[171] ses lèvres. Sa bouche se ferma, et encore une fois ses yeux. Il se redressa. Ses mains montèrent le long du corps, se livrèrent à la hauteur du visage à un incompréhensible manège,[172] qui ressemblait à certaines figures des danses religieuses de Java. Puis il se prit les tempes et le front, écrasant ses paupières sous les petits doigts allongés.

«Ils m'ont dit: «C'est notre droit et notre devoir.» Notre devoir! Heureux celui qui trouve avec une aussi simple certitude la route de son devoir!»

Ses mains retombèrent.

«Au carrefour,[173] on vous dit: «Prenez cette route-là.» Il secoua la tête. «Or, cette route, on ne la voit pas s'élever vers les hauteurs lumineuses des cimes,[174] on la voit descendre vers une vallée sinistre, s'enfoncer dans les ténèbres fétides d'une lugubre[175] forêt!... O Dieu! Montrez-moi où est MON devoir!»

Il dit, – il cria presque:

«C'est le Combat, – le Grand Bataille du Temporel contre le Spirituel!»

Il regardait, avec une fixité lamentable l'ange de bois sculpté au-dessus de la fenêtre, l'ange extatique et souriant, lumineux de tranquillité céleste.

Soudain son expression sembla se détendre.[176] Le corps perdit de sa raideur. Son visage s'inclina un peu vers le sol. Il le releva:

«J'ai fait valoir mes droits, dit-il avec naturel. J'ai demandé à

"Not like wax, but like the plaster of certain delapidated walls: gray with more whitish spots of saltpeter."

    délabrés: dilapidated

    salpêtre: saltpeter

170. *farouche*: wild
171. *franchit*: crossed
172. *manège*: merry-go-round
173. *au carrefour*: at the intersection
174. *cimes*: heights; summits
175. *lugubre*: dismal
176. *se détendre*: to relax

rejoindre une division en campagne. Cette faveur m'a été enfin accordée: demain, je suis autorisé à me mettre en route.»

Je crus voir flotter sur ses lèvres un fantôme de sourire quand il précisa:

«Pour l'enfer.»

Son bras se leva vers l'Orient, – vers ces plaines immenses où le blé futur sera nourri de cadavres.

Je pensai: «Ainsi il se soumet. Voilà donc tout ce qu'ils savent faire. Ils se soumettent tous. Même cet homme-là.»

Le visage de ma nièce me fit peine. Il était d'une pâleur lunaire. Les lèvres, pareilles aux bords d'un vase d'opaline, étaient disjointes, elles esquissaient la moue tragique des masques grecs. Et je vis, à la limite du front et de la chevelure, non pas naître, mais jaillir, – oui, jaillir, – des perles de sueur.[177]

Je ne sais si Werner von Ebrennac le vit. Ses pupilles, celles de la jeune fille, amarrées[178] comme, dans le courant, la barque à l'anneau de la rive, semblaient l'être par un fil si tendu, si raide, qu'on n'eût pas osé passer un doigt entre leurs yeux. Ebrennac d'une main avait saisi le bouton de la porte. De l'autre il tenait le chambranle.[179] Sans bouger son regard d'une ligne, il tira lentement la porte à lui. Il dit, – sa voix était étrangement dénuée d'expression:[180]

«Je vous souhaite une bonne nuit.»

Je crus qu'il allait fermer la porte et partir. Mais non. Il regardait ma nièce. Il la regardait. Il dit, – il murmura:

«Adieu.»

Il ne bougea pas. Il restait tout à fait immobile, et dans son visage immobile et tendu, les yeux étaient plus encore immobiles et tendus, attachés aux yeux, – trop ouverts, trop pâles, – de ma nièce. Cela dura, dura, – combien de temps? – dura jusqu'à ce qu'enfin, la jeune fille remuât les lèvres.[181] Les yeux de Werner brillèrent.

---

177. *esquissaient la moue tragique*: formed the tragic pout
   jaillir: spout out; surge forth
   des perles de sueur: pearls of sweat
"They outline the tragic pout of Greek masks. And I saw, at the hairline, pearls of sweat, not forming, but surging forth, – yes, surging forth."
178. *amarrées*: moored
179. *le chambranle*: the doorframe
180. *dénuée d'expression*: devoid of expression
181. *remuât les lèvres*: moved her lips

J'entendis:

«Adieu.»

Il fallait avoir guetté[182] ce mot pour l'entendre, mais enfin je l'entendis. Von Ebrennac aussi l'entendit, et il se redressa, et son visage et tout son corps semblèrent s'assoupir[183] comme après un bain reposant.

Et il sourit, de sorte que la dernière image que j'eus de lui fut une image souriante. Et la porte se ferma et ses pas s'évanouirent[184] au fond de la maison.

Il était parti quand, le lendemain, je descendis prendre ma tasse de lait matinale. Ma nièce avait préparé le déjeuner, comme chaque jour. Elle me servit en silence. Nous bûmes en silence. Dehors luisait au travers de la brume un pâle soleil. Il me sembla qu'il faisait très froid.

Octobre 1941

---

182. *avoir guetté*: to have been on the lookout for
183. *s'assoupir*: to relax
184. *s'évanouirent*: vanished

The Silence of the Sea
I

To the memory of SAINT-POL-ROUX the murdered poet[1]

There was a great display of military preparations before he
arrived. First came two troopers, both very fair; one thin and
gangling, the other squarely built with the hands of a quarryman.
They looked at my house without going in. Later an N.C.O.[2]
arrived, and the gangling trooper went with him. They spoke to
me in what they thought was French, but I didn't understand a
word. However, I showed them the unoccupied rooms and they
seemed satisfied.

Next morning an enormous grey army touring-car drove into
my garden. The driver and a slim, fair-haired, smiling young
soldier extricated two packing-cases from it, plus a large bundle
wrapped up in grey cloth. They took the whole lot up to the largest
room. The car went away, and a few hours later I heard hoofbeats.
Three horsemen appeared. One dismounted and went off to have a
look at the old stone building. When he came back all, men and
horses alike, went into the barn which I use as my workroom. I
saw later that they had driven the clamp from my carpenter's bench
between two stones, in a hole in the wall, fastened a rope to the
clamp and tied the horses to the rope.

For two days nothing more happened. I never saw a soul. The
troopers went out early with their horses; in the evening they
brought them back, and then they went to bed in the straw with
which they had stuffed the attic.

Then, on the morning of the third day, the big touring-car
returned. The smiling young man heaved a large officer's suitcase
on his shoulder and carried it up to the room. Then he took his
kitbag which he put in the room next door. He came downstairs

---

1. Pseudonym for Paul Roux (1861–1940), symbolist poet; see Vercors, *Battle of
Silence*, p. 169: "The Germans had invaded his house, shot down his housekeeper
before his eyes, seriously wounded his daughter Divine and set the whole house on
fire; his own skull split by a rifle-butt, he had succumbed to the effects of this
savagery in hospital at Brest."
2. Noncommissioned officer (for example, sergeant).

and, speaking in good French to my niece, asked her for some sheets.

It was my niece who went to open the door when there was a knock. She had just brought me my coffee, as she did every evening (coffee helps me to sleep), and I was sitting in the back of the room in comparative darkness. The door opens straight on to the garden, and all round the house runs a red-tiled path which is very useful when it is wet. We heard footsteps and the sound of heels on the tiles. My niece looked at me and put down her cup. I kept mine in my hands.

It was night, but not very cold; all that November it was never very cold. I could see a massive figure, a flat cap, a mackintosh thrown round the shoulders like a cape.

My niece had opened the door and was waiting in silence. She had pulled the door right back to the wall and was standing up against the wall not looking at anything. For my part, I was drinking my coffee in little sips.

"If you please," said the officer in the doorway. He gave a little nod of greeting and seemed to be gauging the depth of the silence. Then he came in.

He slid the cape onto his arm, gave a military salute, and took off his cap; then he turned to my niece and, with a quiet smile, made her a very slight bow. Then he faced me and made me a deeper bow. "My name," he said, "is Werner von Ebrennac." I had time for the thought to cross my mind quickly: That's not a German name; perhaps he is descended from a Protestant émigré.[3] Then he added, "I am extremely sorry."

The last word, which he drawled slightly, fell into the silence. My niece had closed the door and was still leaning against the wall looking straight in front of her. I hadn't got up. Slowly I put down my empty cup on the harmonium, then crossed my hands and waited.

The officer went on. "It had to be done, of course. I would have avoided it if I could. I am sure my orderly will do his best not to

3. "This name of Gascon Huguenot origin, which was my own invention entirely, cannot be very common in Germany. . . . If the authors of *Is Paris Burning?* are to be believed, the officer in charge of blowing up the bridges [in the capital during the German withdrawal in the summer of 1944] was called Ebrennac." See Vercors, *Battle of Silence*, p. 280; but also Larry Collins and Dominique Lapierre, *Is Paris Burning?* (New York, 1965), pp. 71–73, 77–78, 211, 220, 235, 261, where the officer in question is identified as "Captain Werner Ebernach."

disturb you." He was standing in the middle of the room, huge and very thin; he could easily touch the beams by raising his arm. His head was hanging forward a little as if his neck didn't grow out from his shoulders, but from the top of his chest. He wasn't round-shouldered, but it looked as if he were. His narrow shoulders and hips were most striking, and his face was handsome; it was very masculine, and there were two big hollows in his cheeks. I couldn't see his eyes, which were hidden in the shadow of his brow, but they seemed light-coloured; his hair was fair and smooth, brushed straight back and giving out a silky glitter under the chandelier.

The silence was unbroken, it grew closer and closer like the morning mist; it was thick and motionless. The immobility of my niece, and for that matter my own, made it even heavier, turned it to lead. The officer himself, taken aback, stood without moving till at last I saw the beginning of a smile on his lips. His smile was serious and without a trace of irony. With his hand he made a vague gesture whose meaning I did not grasp, and fixed his eyes on my niece, still standing there stiffly, so that I had leisure to examine his strong profile, his thin and prominent nose. I saw a gold tooth shining between his half-closed lips. He turned his eyes away at last, stared at the fire on the hearth, and said, "I feel a very deep respect for people who love their country." Then he raised his head abruptly and looked at the carved angel over the window. "I could go up to my room now," he said, "but I don't know the way." My niece opened the door which gives on to the back staircase and began to climb the steps, without looking at the officer, just as if she had been alone. The officer followed her, and it was then I noticed that he was lame in one leg. I heard them cross the anteroom; the German's steps, a strong one, then a weak one, echoed down the corridor. A door opened and closed again; then my niece came back. She picked up her cup and went on drinking her coffee. I lit my pipe, and for a few minutes neither of us spoke; then I said, "Thank the Lord he looks fairly decent." My niece shrugged her shoulders. She took my velvet jacket on her lap and finished the piece of invisible mending which she had begun.

Next morning the officer came down while we were having breakfast in the kitchen. Another staircase leads to it, and I don't know if the German heard us or if he came that way by accident.

He stopped in the doorway and said, "I have had a very good night. I should hope yours was as good as mine." He looked round the huge room with a smile. As we had very little wood and less coal, I had repainted it, we had brought in some furniture, some copper pans and old plates, so as to shut ourselves in there for the winter. All that, he took in, and we caught the gleam of the edge of his very white teeth. I saw that his eyes were not blue, as I had thought, but a golden brown. At last he crossed the room and opened the door on to the garden. He took a couple of steps and turned back to inspect our long low house with its ancient brown tiles and its covering of creepers.[4] His smile broadened. "Your old mayor had told me I was to stay at the Château," he said, pointing with a backward flick of his hand at the pretentious building which could be seen a little higher up the hill, through the bare trees. "I shall congratulate my men on their mistake. Here it is a much more beautiful château." Then he closed the door, saluted us through the window pane, and disappeared.

That evening he came back at the same time as before. We were having our coffee. He knocked but didn't wait for my niece to open the door; he opened it himself. "I am afraid I am disturbing you," he said. "If you would rather, I will come in through the kitchen; then you can keep this door locked." He crossed the room and stopped a moment with his hand on the doorknob, looking into the various corners of the smoking-room. Then he made a slight bow. "I wish you a very good night," he said, and went out.

We never locked the door. I am not sure that our motives for this omission were very clear or unmixed. By a silent agreement, my niece and I had decided to make no changes in our life, not even in the smallest detail – as if the officer didn't exist, as if he had been a ghost. But it's possible that there was another sentiment mixed with this wish in my heart: I can't hurt anyone's feelings, even my enemy's, without suffering myself.[5]

For a long time, for more than a month in fact, the same scene took place every day. The officer knocked and came in. He spoke a few words about the weather, the temperature, or some other subject equally unimportant: all that these remarks had in common was that they did not call for an answer. He always lingered a moment on the threshold of the little door, and looked around him.

4. The Bruller family's house; see Vercors, *Battle of Silence*, pp. 151, 165.
5. For the expression of a similar sentiment by Bruller see *Battle of Silence*, pp. 120–21.

A ghost of a smile would betray the pleasure which he seemed to get from this examination – the same examination every day, and the same pleasure. His eyes would rest on the bowed profile of my niece, invariably severe and impassive, and when at last he took his eyes off her I was sure I could read in them a kind of smiling approval. Then he would say with a bow as he left, "I wish you a very good night."

One evening everything changed abruptly. Outside, a fine snow mixed with rain was falling, terribly cold and damping. On the hearth I was burning the heavy logs which I kept especially for nights like this. In spite of myself I kept imagining the officer outside and how powdered he would be with snow when he came in. But he never came. It was much beyond his usual time, and it annoyed me to realize how my thoughts were taken up with him. My niece was knitting slowly, with a concentrated air.

At last we heard steps, but they came from inside the house. I recognized the unequal tread of the officer, and I realized that he had come in by the other door and was now on his way from his room. No doubt he hadn't wanted to appear before us unimpressive in a wet uniform, and so he had changed first.

The steps, a strong one, then a weak one, came down the staircase. The door opened, and there was the officer. He was in mufti, and was wearing a pair of thick grey flannel trousers and a steel-blue tweed coat with a warm brown check. It was large and loose-fitting and hung with easy carelessness. Beneath his coat a cream woollen pull-over fitted tightly over his spare and muscular body.

"Excuse me," he said. "I'm feeling cold. I got wet through, and my room is very chilly. I will warm myself at your fire for a few minutes." With some difficulty he crouched down by the hearth, put out his hands, and kept on turning them round. "That's fine," he said, and moved round to warm his back at the fire, still squatting and clasping one knee in his hands.

"Here it's nothing," he said. 'Winter in France is a mild season. Where I come from, it's very hard. Very. The trees are all firs, close-packed forests with the snow heavy on them. Here the trees are delicate, and the snow on them is like lace. My home reminds me of a powerful thickset bull which needs all its strength to keep alive. Here everything is intelligence, and subtle poetic thought."

His voice was rather colourless, with very little resonance, and his accent was fairly slight, only noticeable on the harsher consonants. The general effect was of a kind of musical buzzing. He got up and rested his arm on the top of the high chimneypiece, leaning his forehead on the back of his hand. He was so tall that he had to stoop a little, whereas I shouldn't even have caught the top of my head there. He remained for a long time without moving or saying anything. My niece was knitting with machinelike energy, nor did she once look up at him. I was smoking, half stretched out in my big soft armchair. I imagined that nothing could disturb the weight of our silence, that the man would bid us good-night and go. But the muffled and musical buzzing began again; one couldn't say that it broke the silence, for it seemed to be born out of it.

"I have always loved France," said the officer without moving. "Always. I was only a child in the last war, and what I thought then doesn't count. But ever since I have always loved it – only it was from a distance, like the Princesse Lointaine."[6] He paused before saying solemnly, "Because of my father."

He turned round with his hands in his coat-pockets and leant against the side of the chimneypiece; he kept bumping his head a little against the shelf. From time to time he slowly rubbed the back of his head against it with a natural movement, like a stag's. An armchair was there for him just at hand, but he didn't sit down. Right up to the last day he never sat down. We never gave, nor did he ever take, anything remotely like an opening for familiarity.

"Because of my father," he repeated. "He was intensely patriotic. The defeat was a great blow to him. And yet he loved France. He liked Briand,[7] he believed in the Weimar Republic[8] and in Briand, and he was very enthusiastic. He used to say, 'He is going to unite us like husband and wife.' He thought the sun was going to rise over Europe at last."

While he was talking he was watching my niece. He did not look at her as a man looks at a woman, but as he looks at a statue. And a statue was exactly what she was – a living one, but a statue all the same.

"But Briand was defeated. My father saw that France was still led by your heartless *grands bourgeois* – by people like your De

6. Play by Edmond Rostand (1868–1918), published in 1895.

7. Aristide Briand (1862–1932), Socialist premier and foreign minister during the 1920s, advocate of reconciliation with Germany, cowinner of the Nobel Peace Prize in 1926 with German foreign minister Gustav Stresemann.

8. Unofficial name for the democratic government of Germany from 1918/19 to January 1933, succeeded by the Nazi Third Reich.

Wendels,[9] your Henri Bordeaux,[10] and your old Marshal.[11] He said to me, 'You must never go to France till you can do it in field-boots and a helmet.' I had to promise him that, for he was nearly dying, and when war broke out I knew the whole of Europe except France."

He smiled, and said, as if that had been a reason:

"I am a musician, you see."

A log fell in, and some embers rolled out from the hearth. The German leant over and picked up the embers with the tongs; then he went on:

"I am not a performer. I am a composer. That is my whole life, and so it's comical for me to see myself as a man of war. And yet I don't regret this war. No. I think that great things will come of it."

He straightened himself, took his hands out of his pockets and half raised them.

"Forgive me: I may have said something to hurt you. But I was saying what I think, and with sincere good feeling. I feel it because of my love of France. Great things will come of it for Germany and for France. I think, as my father did, that the sun is going to shine over Europe."

He took a couple of steps and bowed slightly. As on every evening he said, "I wish you a very good night." Then he went away.

I finished my pipe in silence, then I coughed slightly and said, "It's perhaps too unkind to refuse him even a farthing's worth of answer." My niece lifted her head. She raised her eyebrows very high, her eyes were shining with indignation.

Almost I felt myself blushing.

From that day his visits took on a new shape. Very rarely indeed did we see him in uniform; he used to change first and then knock on our door. Was it to spare us the sight of the uniform of the

9. France's leading family of iron and steel manufacturers, prominently represented in economic organizations at Vichy.

10. Writer (1870–1963) whose novels celebrated traditional values of family and religion, and who while serving as an official military historian in the First World War became a confidant of Marshal Pétain.

11. Henri Philippe Pétain (1856–1951), defender of Verdun and army commander in chief during World War I, war minister in 1934, ambassador to Franco's Spain after 1939, from the French defeat in the summer of 1940 until the liberation of France four years later Chief of State in the initially unoccupied southern zone with its capital at Vichy; after the war tried for treason and condemned to death, but the sentence was commuted by General de Gaulle to life imprisonment.

enemy? or to make us forget it, to get us used to his personality? No doubt a bit of both. He used to knock, and then he would come in without waiting for the answer which he knew we would not give. He did it in the simplest and most natural way, and would warm himself at the fire, which was the excuse he always gave for his arrival – an excuse by which none of us was taken in, and whose useful conventionality he made no attempt to disguise.

He did not come every evening without fail; but I do not remember a single one in which he did not talk to us before he left. He used to lean over the fire, and while he was warming some part or other of himself at the blaze his droning voice would quietly make itself heard and, for the rest of the evening, there was an interminable monologue on the subjects – his country, music, France – which were obsessing his mind; for not once did he try to get an answer from us, or a sign of agreement or even a glance. He used not to speak for long – never for much longer than on the first evening. He would pronounce a few sentences, sometimes broken by silences, and sometimes linking them up with the monotonous continuity of a prayer; sometimes he leant against the chimneypiece without moving, like a caryatid; sometimes, without interrupting himself, he would go up to an object or a drawing on the wall. Then he would be silent, bow to us, and wish us a good night.

One day he said (it was in the early stages of his visits): "What is the difference between the fire in my home and this one here? Certainly the wood, the flame, and the fireplace are exactly alike. But not the light. That depends on the things on which it shines – the people in this smoking-room, the furniture, the walls, and the books on their shelves . . .

"Why am I so fond of this room?" he went on thoughtfully. "It's not particularly beautiful – Oh, excuse me!" he laughed. "I mean to say it's not a museum piece . . . Take your furniture: it does not make one say, 'What lovely things!' No. And yet this room has a soul. All this house has a soul!"

He was standing in front of the shelves of the bookcase, and with a light touch his fingers were fondling the bindings.

"Balzac, Barrès, Baudelaire, Beaumarchais, Boileau, Buffon . . ."[12]

12. Honoré de Balzac (1799–1850), novelist; Maurice Barrès (1862–1923), novelist and nationalist politician; Charles Baudelaire (1821–1867), poet and literary critic; Pierre Augustin Caron de Beaumarchais (1732–1799), dramatist; Nicolas Boileau-Despréaux (1636–1711), literary critic and poet; Georges Louis Leclerc, comte de Buffon (1707–1788), naturalist and author.

Chateaubriand, Corneille, Descartes, Fénelon, Flaubert . . .[13] La Fontaine, France, Gautier, Hugo . . .[14] What a roll-call!" he said, shaking his head with a little laugh, "and I've only got as far as the letter 'H'! Not to Molière, nor Rabelais, nor Racine, nor Pascal, nor Stendhal, nor Voltaire, nor Montaigne,[15] nor any of the others!" He went on slowly moving along the bookshelves, and from time to time he muttered an exclamation, I suppose when he came to a name which he had not expected. "With the English," he went on, "one immediately thinks of Shakespeare; with the Italians, it is Dante. Spain: Cervantes. And with us at once: Goethe.[16] After that one has to stop and consider. But if someone says, 'And France?' then who comes to the tip of one's tongue? Molière? Racine? Hugo? Voltaire? Rabelais? Or which of the others? They jostle each other like the crowd at the entrance to a theatre till you don't know which to let in first."

He turned round, adding in all solemnity, "But when it comes to music, then it's our turn: Bach, Händel, Beethoven, Wagner, Mozart . . .[17] Which name comes first?"

"And now we are at war with each other," he said slowly, shaking his head. He had come back to the fireplace, and he let his eyes rest smiling on my niece's profile. "But this is the last time! We won't fight each other any more. We'll get married!" His eyelids crinkled, the hollows under his cheekbones went into two

13. François René, vicomte de Chateaubriand (1768–1848), writer and founder of romanticism; Pierre Corneille (1606–1684), classical dramatist; René Descartes (1596–1650), scientist and philosopher; François de Salignac de la Mothe Fénelon (1651–1715), theologian and writer; Gustave Flaubert (1821–1880), realist novelist.

14. Jean de La Fontaine (1621–1695), poet and author of fables; Anatole France (1844–1924), novelist and winner of the Nobel Prize for literature in 1921; Théophile Gautier (1811–1872), novelist, poet, and art critic; Victor-Marie, vicomte Hugo (1802–1885), dramatist, poet, and novelist.

15. Jean-Baptiste Poquelin Molière (1622–1673), playwright and actor; François Rabelais (ca. 1490–1533), comic writer and physician; Jean Racine (1639–1699), classical dramatist; Blaise Pascal (1623–1662), scientist and religious philosopher; Marie-Henri Beyle, pseud. Stendhal (1783–1842), novelist; François-Marie Arouet de Voltaire (1694–1778), philosopher and writer; Michel Eyquem, seigneur de Montaigne (1533–1592), essayist.

16. William Shakespeare (1564–1616), Dante Alighieri (1265–1321), Miguel de Cervantes Saavedra (1547–1616), Johann Wolfgang von Goethe (1749–1832): the foremost dramatists, poets, and novelists of England, Italy, Spain, and Germany respectively.

17. Johann Sebastian Bach (1685–1750), George Frederic Händel (1685–1759), Ludwig van Beethoven (1770–1827), Richard Wagner (1813–1883), Wolfgang Amadeus Mozart (1756–1791): German-born composers and musicians.

long furrows and he showed his white teeth. "Yes, yes," he said gaily, and a little toss of the head repeated this affirmation. "When we entered Saintes,"[18] he went on after a silence, "I was happy that the population received us well. I was very happy. I thought: This is going to be easy. And then I saw that it was not that at all, that it was cowardice." He became serious again. "I despised those people, and for France's sake I was afraid. I thought: Has she *really* got like that?" He shook his head. "No, no, I have seen her since, and now I am happy at her stern expression."

His gaze fell on mine. I looked away. It hesitated for a little at various points in the room and then turned again on the unrelentingly expressionless face which it had left.

"I am happy to have found here an elderly man with some dignity, and a young lady who knows how to be silent. We have got to conquer this silence. We have got to conquer the silence of all France. I am glad of that."

Silently, and with a grave insistence which still carried the hint of a smile, he was looking at my niece, at her closed, obstinate, delicate profile. My niece felt it, and I saw her blush slightly, and a little frown form gradually between her eyebrows. Her fingers plucked the needle perhaps rather too quickly and tartly, at the risk of breaking the thread.

"Yes," went on his slow, droning voice. "It's better that way. Much better. That makes for a solid union – for unions where both sides gain in greatness . . . There is a very lovely children's story which I have read, which you have read, which everybody has read. I don't know if it has the same title in both countries. With us it's called 'Das Tier und die Schöne' – 'Beauty and the Beast.' Poor Beauty! The Beast holds her at his pleasure, captive and powerless – at every hour of the day he forces his oppressive and relentless presence on her . . . Beauty is all pride and dignity – she has hardened her heart . . . But the Beast is something better than he seems. Oh, he's not very polished, he's clumsy and brutal, he seems very uncouth beside his exquisite Beauty! But he has a heart. Yes, he has a heart which hopes to raise itself up . . . If Beauty only *would*! But it is a long time before Beauty will. However, little by little she discovers the light at the back of the eyes of her hated jailer – the light which reveals his supplication and his love. She is less

18. Town in western France on the Charente River, Department Charente-Maritime.

conscious of his heavy hand and of the chains of her prison . . . She ceases to hate him. His constancy moves her, she gives him her hand . . . At once the Beast is transformed, the spell which has kept him in that brutish hide is broken: and now behold a handsome and chivalrous knight, sensitive and cultivated, whom every kiss from his Beauty adorns with more and more shining qualities! Their union gives them the most perfect happiness. Their children, who combine and mingle the gifts of their parents, are the loveliest the earth has borne . . .

"Weren't you fond of this story? For my part, I always loved it. I have reread it over and over again. It used to make me cry. I loved the Beast above all because I understood his misery. Even today I am moved when I speak of it."

He was silent, then he took a deep breath and bowed.

"I wish you a very good night!"

One evening when I had gone up into my room to look for my tobacco I heard someone playing the harmonium: playing the "Eighth Prelude and Fugue,"[19] which my niece had been practising before the catastrophe. The score had remained open at that page, but up to the evening in question my niece had not been able to bring herself to go on with it. That she had begun again caused me both pleasure and astonishment: what deep inward need could have made her change her mind so suddenly? But it was not my niece – for she had not left her armchair or her work. Her eyes met mine and sent me a message which I could not decipher. I looked at the long back bowed over the instrument, the bent neck, the long, delicate, nervous hands whose fingers changed places over the keys as rapidly as if they had each a life of their own.

He only played the Prelude, then he got up and came back to the fire.

"There is nothing greater than that," he said in his low voice, which was hardly more than a whisper. "Great – that's not quite the word. Outside man – outside human flesh. That makes us understand, no, not understand but guess . . . No: have a presentiment . . . have a presentiment of what nature is . . . of what – stripped bare – is the divine and unknowable nature of the human soul. Yes, it's inhuman music."

19. By J.S. Bach.

He seemed to be following out his own train of thought in a dreaming silence; he was slowly biting his lip.

"Bach . . . he could only be a German. Our country has that character; that inhuman character. I mean – by 'inhuman' – that which is on a different scale to man."

Then, after a pause:

"That kind of music – I love it, I admire it, it overwhelms me; it's like the presence of God in me . . . but it's not my own.

"For my part, I would like to compose music which is on the scale of man; that also is a road by which one can reach the truth. That's *my* road. I don't want to follow any other, and besides I couldn't. That, I know now; I know it to the full. Since when? Since I have lived here."

He turned his back on us and leant his hands on the mantelpiece. He gripped it with his fingers and held his face towards the fire through his forearms, as if through the bars of a grating. His voice became lower and even more droning.

"Now I really need France. But I ask a great deal; I ask a welcome from her. To be here as a stranger, as a traveller or a conqueror, that's nothing. France gives nothing then, for there is nothing one can take from her. Her riches, her true riches, one can't conquer; one can only drink them in at her breast. She has to offer you her breast, like a mother, in a movement of maternal feeling . . . I know that that depends on us . . . but it depends on her too. She must consent to understand our thirst, she must consent to quench it, and she must consent to unite herself with us."

He stood up, his back still turned to us, his fingers still gripping the stone. "As for me," he said a little more loudly, "I must live here for a long time. In a house like this one. As a child of a village like this village . . . I must . . ."

He was silent. He turned towards us. He smiled with his mouth, but not with his eyes, which were looking at my niece.

"We will overcome all obstacles," he said. "Sincerity is bound to overcome all obstacles."

"I wish you a very good night!"

I can't remember today everything that was said during the course of more than a hundred winter evenings, but the theme hardly ever varied; it was the long rhapsody of his discovery of France: how he had loved her from afar before he came to know her, and how his love had grown every day since he had had the luck to live there. And believe me, I admired him for it. Yes, because nothing seemed to discourage him, and because he never tried to shake off our inexorable silence by any violent expression . . . On the contrary, when he sometimes let the silence invade the whole room and, like a heavy unbreathable gas, saturate every corner of it, of the three of us it was he who used to seem most at ease. Then he would look at my niece with that expression of approval which was both solemn and smiling at the same time, and which he had kept ever since his first day, and I would feel the spirit of my niece being troubled in that prison which she had herself built for it. I would notice it by several signs, of which the least was a faint fluttering of her fingers, and so when at last Werner von Ebrennac set the silence draining away gently and smoothly with his droning voice, he seemed to make it possible for me to breathe more freely.

He would often talk about himself: "My house is in the forest; I was born there; I used to go to the village school on the other side; I never left home until I went to Munich for my examinations, and to Salzburg for the music. I've lived there ever since. I don't like big cities. I know London, Vienna, Rome, Warsaw, and, of course, the German towns, but I would not like to live in any of them. The only place I really liked was Prague – no other city has such a soul. And above all Nuremberg.[20] For a German it is the city which makes his heart swell because there he finds the ghosts which are dear to his soul. Every stone is a reminder of those who made the glory of the old Germany. I think the French must feel the same thing before the Cathedral of Chartres.[21] There they too must feel the presence of their ancestors beside them, the beauty of their spirit, the greatness of their faith, and all their graciousness. Fate led me to Chartres. Oh, truly, when it appears over the ripe corn, blue in the distance, transparent, ethereal, it stirs one's heart! I imagined the feelings of those who used to go there on foot, on horseback or by wagon in the olden time. I shared their feelings, and I loved those people. How I wish I could be their brother!"

His face grew stern: "No doubt it's hard to believe that of

20. See Bruller's account of his 1938 visit to this medieval German city in *Battle of Silence*, pp. 33–34.
21. Town southwest of Paris on the Eure River, Department Eure-et-Loir; famous for its Gothic cathedral with twin spires, stained glass windows, and sculpture.

somebody who arrived at Chartres in a huge armoured car; but all the same it's the truth. So many things are going on at the same time in the heart of a German, even the best German! Things of which he would so gladly be cured." He smiled again, a faint smile which slowly lit up all his face; then he said:

"In the country house nearest my home there lives a young girl. She is very beautiful and very sweet. My father at any rate would have been very glad if I had married her. When he died we were practically engaged, and they used to let us go out for long walks alone together."

My niece had just snapped her thread, and before going on he waited until she had threaded her needle again. She did it with great concentration, but the eye of the needle was very small and it was no easy matter. Finally she succeeded.

"One day," he went on, "we were in the forest. Rabbits and squirrels scampered before us. All kinds of flowers were there, narcissus, wild hyacinth, and amaryllis. The young girl cried out in her joy. She said, 'I'm so happy, Werner. I love, oh, how I love these gifts from God!' I too was happy. We lay down on the moss in the midst of the bracken. We did not say a word. Above our heads we saw the tops of the fir trees swaying and the birds flying from branch to branch. The young girl gave a little cry: 'Oh, he's stung me on the chin! Dirty little beast, nasty little mosquito!' Then I saw her make a quick grab with her hand. 'I have caught one, Werner! Oh, look, I'm going to punish him: I'm – pulling – his – legs – off – one – after – the – other . . .' And she did so . . .[22]

"Luckily," he went on, "she had plenty of other suitors. I did not feel any remorse, but at the same time I was scared away for ever where German girls were concerned."

He looked thoughtfully at the inside of his hands and said:

"And that's what our politicians are like too. That's why I never wanted to associate with them in spite of my friends who wrote to me: 'Come and join us.' No: I preferred to stay at home always. It wasn't a good thing for the success of my music, but no matter: success is a very little thing compared to a quiet conscience. And indeed I know very well that my friends and our Führer[23] have the grandest and the noblest conceptions, but I know equally well that

22. A German nurse in the employ of the Bruller family performed a similar action; see Vercors, *Battle of Silence*, p. 151.

23. Leader, that is, Adolf Hitler (1889–1945), chancellor of Germany from 1933 until his death by suicide.

they would pull mosquitoes' legs off, one after the other. That's what always happens with Germans when they are very lonely: it always comes up to the top. And who are more lonely than men of the same Party[24] when they are in power?"

"Happily they are now alone no longer: they are in France. France will cure them, and I'm going to tell you the truth: they know it. They know that France will teach them how to be really great and pure in heart."

He went towards the door and said, swallowing his words as if talking to himself:

"But for that we must have love."

He held the door open for a moment and, looking over his shoulder, he gazed at my niece's neck as she leant over her work, at the pale, fragile nape of her neck whence the hair went up in coils of dark mahogany, and then he added in a tone of quiet determination:

"A love which is returned."

Then he turned his head, and the door closed on him as he rapidly uttered his evening formula:

"I wish you a very good night."

The long spring days came at last, and now the officer came down with the last rays of the setting sun. He still wore his grey flannel trousers, but he had on his shoulders a lighter woollen jacket, the colour of rough homespun, over a linen shirt with an open neck. One evening he came down holding a book with his forefinger closed in it. His face brightened with that half-withheld smile which foreshadows the pleasure we are confident of giving others. He said:

"I brought this down for you. It's a page of *Macbeth*. Ye gods, what greatness!"

He opened the book:

"It's at the end. Macbeth's power is slipping through his fingers, and with it the loyalty of those who have grasped at last the blackness of his ambition. The noble lords who are defending the honour of Scotland are awaiting his imminent overthrow. One of them describes the dramatic portents of this collapse . . ."

And he read slowly, with a pathetic heaviness:

24. National Socialist German Workers' Party (NSDAP or Nazis).

"Now does he feel
His secret murders sticking on his hands;
Now minutely revolts upbraid his faith-breach;
Those he commands move only in command,
Nothing in love: now does he feel his title
Hang loose about him, like a giant's robe
Upon a dwarfish thief."

He raised his head and laughed. I wondered with stupefaction if he was thinking of the same tyrant as I was, but he said:

"Isn't that just what must be keeping your Admiral[25] awake at night? I really pity that man in spite of the contempt which he inspires in me as much as in you."

"Those he commands move only in command,
Nothing in love . . ."

"A leader who has not his people's love is a very miserable little puppet. Only . . . only, could one expect anything else? Who in fact except some dreary climber of that kind could have taken on such a part? And yet it had to be. Yes, there had to be someone who would agree to sell his country, because today – today and for a long time to come – France cannot fall willingly into our open arms without losing her dignity in her own eyes. Often the most sordid go-between is thus at the bottom of the happiest union. The go-between is none the less contemptible for that, nor is the union less happy."

He closed the book with a snap and stuffed it in his coat pocket, mechanically giving the pocket a couple of slaps with the palm of his hand. Then he said with a cheerful expression lighting up his long face:

"I have to inform my hosts that I shall be away for a couple of weeks. I am overjoyed to be going to Paris. It's now my turn for leave, and I shall spend it in Paris for the first time. This is a great day for me. It's my greatest day until the coming of another one, for which I hope with all my heart, and which will be an even

25. Jean François Darlan (1881–1942), commander in chief of the French navy in 1939 and first naval, then (February 1941 to April 1942) foreign minister, vice-premier, and successor-designate to Marshal Pétain in the Vichy government; he ordered resistance to the Allied invasion of France's North African territories in November 1942 to cease but was assassinated a month later.

greater day. I shall know how to wait for years if necessary. My heart knows how to be patient."

"I expect I shall see my friends in Paris, where many of them have come for the negotiations which we are conducting with your politicians to prepare for the wonderful union of our two countries. So I shall be in a way a witness to the marriage . . . I want to tell you that I am happy for the sake of France, whose wounds will thus be so quickly healed, but I am even happier for Germany and for myself. No one will ever have gained so much from a good deed as will Germany by giving back to France her greatness and her liberty!"

"I wish you a very good night."

II

We did not set eyes on him when he came back.

We knew he was there (there are many signs which betray the presence of a guest in the house, even when he remains invisible). But for a number of days – much more than a week – we never saw him.

Shall I admit it? His absence did not leave my mind at peace. I thought of him, I don't know how far it wasn't with regret or anxiety. Neither I nor my niece spoke of him. But in the evening when we sometimes heard the dull echo of his uneven step upstairs I could clearly see from her sudden obstinate busying with her work, from the faint lines that gave her face an expression which was both set and expectant, that she was not immune from thoughts like mine.

One day I had to go to the Kommandantur[26] for some business about declaring tires.[27] While I was filling in the form they had given me, Werner von Ebrennac came out of his office. At first he did not see me. He spoke to the sergeant who was sitting at a little table before a long mirror on the wall. I heard the singsong inflection of his low voice, and, although I had nothing more to do, I waited there without knowing why, yet curiously moved, and expecting I know not what climax. I saw his face in the mirror, it seemed pale and drawn. He raised his eyes until they caught my own. For two seconds we stared at each other, then he suddenly turned on his heel and faced me. His lips parted, and slowly he raised his hand a little, then almost immediately let it fall again. He shook his head almost imperceptibly with a kind of pathetic irresolution, as if he had said 'No' to himself, yet never taking his eyes off me. Then he made a very slight bow, as he let his glance fall to the ground, hobbled back into his office, and shut himself in.

I said nothing of this to my niece, but women have a catlike

26. Local German military command headquarters in the occupied northern zone of France.
27. Because rubber for new production was in short supply, the Germans confiscated large numbers of tires in France for their own use.

power of divination; for the whole evening she never stopped lifting her eyes from her work every minute to look at me; to try to read something in my face, which I forced myself to keep expressionless by pulling assiduously at my pipe. In the end she let her hands drop as if tired and, folding up her material, asked if I minded her having an early night. She passed two fingers slowly over her forehead, as if to drive away a headache. She kissed me good-night, and I thought I could read a reproach and a somewhat oppressive sadness in her beautiful grey eyes. After she had gone a ridiculous anger took possession of me: a rage at being ridiculous, and at having a niece who was ridiculous. What was the point of all this nonsense? But I could give no answer to myself. If it was nonsense its roots all the same went very deep.

It was three days later that, just as we were finishing our coffee, we heard the irregular beat of his familiar steps grow clear; and this time they were obviously bent in our direction. I suddenly remembered that winter evening six months ago when we first heard those steps. I thought, And it's raining today too – for it had been raining hard all the morning. A long-drawn, obstinate downpour which drowned everything outside and was even bathing the inside of the house in a cold and clammy atmosphere. My niece had covered her shoulders with a printed silk scarf where ten disturbing hands drawn by Jean Cocteau[28] were limply pointing at each other; as for me, I was warming my hands on the bowl of my pipe – and to think we were in July!

The steps crossed the anteroom and began to make the stairs creak. The man was coming down gradually with a slowness which seemed to increase, not as if a prey to hesitation, but like somebody whose will-power was being strained to the utmost. My niece had raised her head and was looking at me; during all this time she fixed on me the transparent, inhuman stare of a horned owl. And when the last stair creaked, and a long silence followed, her fixed expression vanished, I saw her eyelids grow heavy, her head bend and all her body fall back wearily into the armchair.

I don't believe that the silence lasted more than a few seconds, yet they seemed very long. I felt I could see the man behind the door, with his forefinger raised to knock and yet putting back, putting back the moment when by the mere gesture of knocking he would have to face the future . . . At last he knocked. And it was neither

28. Surrealistic writer, artist, and film-maker (1889–1963).

the gentle knock of someone hesitating nor the sharp knock of nervousness overcome; they were three full, slow knocks, the calm sure knocks that mean a decision from which there is no going back. I expected to see the door open at once as on other occasions, but it remained closed; and then an uncontrollable agitation took possession of me, a medley of questioning and of wavering between conflicting impulses, which every one of the seconds that went by with what seemed to me the increasing velocity of a cataract only made more confused and inextricable. Ought we to answer? Why this sudden change? Why should he expect us this evening to break the silence whose healthy obstinacy had had his full approval, as his behaviour up to now had shown? This evening – this very evening – what was it that our dignity demanded of us?

I looked at my niece to try to catch from her eyes some prompting, some sign, but I met only her side-face. She was watching the handle of the door. She was watching it with that inhuman, owl-like stare which I had noticed already; she was very pale, and I saw her upper lip draw itself tight with pain over the delicate white line of her teeth. For my part, before this inward drama so suddenly revealed to me, something that went so far beyond the mild twinges of my own irresolution, I lost all resistance. At that moment two new knocks came, two only, two quick and gentle knocks, and my niece said, "He is going to leave," in a voice so low and so utterly disheartened that I did not wait any longer and said loudly: "Come in, sir."

Why did I add "sir"? To show that I was asking him in as a man and not as an enemy officer? Or, on the contrary, to show that I knew very well *who* had knocked, and that the words were addressed to him? I don't know, and it doesn't matter. The fact remains that I said "Come in, sir" and that he entered.

I had expected to see him appear in civilian clothes, but he was in uniform. Rather would I say that he was more in uniform than ever, if that will convey that it was quite clear to me that he had donned this attire with the deliberate intention of thrusting it on us. He had pushed the door back to the wall, and he was standing straight up in the doorway, so erect and so stiff that I almost began to doubt if it was the same man in front of me and, for the first time, I noticed how surprisingly he resembled Louis Jouvet, the actor.[29] He stood like that for a few seconds, stiff, straight, and

29. Theatre producer, director, and actor (1887–1951).

silent, his feet a little apart and his arms hanging inert beside his body, his face so cold and so completely impassive that it did not seem as if the slightest emotion could ever dwell there.

But seated as I was deep in my armchair and with my face on a level with his left hand, I noticed that hand; my eyes were caught by that hand, and they stayed there as if chained to it, because of the pathetic spectacle it offered me, and which touchingly belied the man's whole attitude. . . .

I learnt that day that, to anyone who knows how to observe them, the hands can betray emotions as clearly as the face – as well as the face, and better – for they are not so subject to the control of the will. And the fingers of that hand were stretching and bending, were squeezing and clutching, were abandoning themselves to the most violent mimicry, while his face and his whole body remained controlled and motionless.

Then his eyes seemed to come back to life. They rested on me for a moment; I felt as if I had been marked down by a falcon. They were eyes shining between stiff wide-open eyelids, the eyelids, stiff and crumpled at the same time, of a victim to insomnia. Then they rested on my niece – and never left her.

At last his hand grew still, all the fingers bent and clenched in the palm. His mouth opened, and the lips as they separated made a little noise like the uncorking of an empty bottle, then the officer said in a voice that was more toneless than ever:

"I have something very serious to say to you."

My niece sat facing him, but she lowered her head. She twisted round her fingers the wool from her ball, which came unwound as it rolled onto the carpet; this ridiculous task being doubtless the only one that would lend itself to being performed without her giving it a thought – and spare her any shame.

The officer went on – with such a visible effort that it seemed it might be costing him his life:

"Everything that I have said in these six months, everything that the walls of this room have heard . . ." He took a deep breath as laboriously as an asthmatic and kept his lungs full for a moment. "You must . . ." He breathed out again: "You must forget it all."

The girl slowly let her hands fall into the hollow of her skirt where they remained lying helplessly on their sides like boats stranded on the sand; and slowly she raised her head, and then, for the first time – for the very first time – she gave the officer the full gaze of her pale eyes.

He said, so that I scarcely heard him, in less than a whisper, "Oh, welch' ein Licht!"[30] And, as if his eyes were really unable to endure that light, he hid them behind his wrist. Two seconds went by; then he let his hand fall, but he had lowered his eyelids and now it was his turn to keep his gaze fixed on the ground. . . .

His lips made the same little noise, and then he said in a voice that went down, down, down:

"I have seen those men – the victors." Then, after several seconds, in a still lower voice:

"I have spoken to them." And at last in a whisper, slowly and bitterly:

"They laughed at me."

He raised his eyes to me and gravely nodded his head three times, almost imperceptibly. He closed his eyes, then said:

"They said to me: 'Haven't you grasped that we're having them on?' That's what they said. Those very words. 'Wir prellen sie.' They said to me: 'You don't suppose that we're going to be such fools as to let France rise up again on our frontiers? Do you?' They gave a loud laugh and slapped me merrily on the back as they looked at my face: '*We* aren't musicians!' "

As he spoke these last words his voice betrayed an obscure contempt which might have been the reflection of his own feelings towards the others or simply the echo of the very tone in which they had spoken.

"Then I made a long speech – and a spirited one too. They went: 'Tst! Tst!' They answered me: 'Politics aren't a poet's dream. What do you think we went to war for? For the sake of their old Marshal?'[31] They laughed again. 'We're neither madmen nor simpletons: we have the chance to destroy France, and destroy her we will. Not only her material power: her soul as well. Particularly her soul. Her soul is the greatest danger. That's our job at this moment – make no mistake about it, my dear fellow! We'll turn it rotten with our smiles and our consideration. We'll make a grovelling bitch of her.' "

He was silent. He seemed out of breath. He clenched his jaw with such force that I saw his cheekbones stand out and a vein, thick and winding as a worm, beat under his temple. Suddenly all the skin of his face moved in a sort of underground shiver – as a

30. "Oh, what a light!"
31. Pétain.

puff of wind moves a lake; as with the first bubbles the film of cream thickens on the surface of the milk one is boiling. His eyes met the pale, wide-open eyes of my niece, and he said in a low voice, level, intense, and constrained, almost too overburdened to move:

"There is no hope." And in a voice which was even lower, more slow and more toneless, as if to torture himself with the intolerable but established fact: "No hope. No hope." Then suddenly in a voice which was unexpectedly loud and strong and, to my surprise, clear and ringing as a trumpet call, as a cry: "No hope!"

After that, silence.

I thought I heard him laugh. His forehead, racked with anguish, was as wrinkled as a hawser. His lips trembled – the pale yet fevered lips of a sick man.

"They reproached me, they were rather angry with me: 'There you are, you see! You see how infatuated you are with her. There's the real danger! But we'll rid Europe of this pest! We'll purge it of this poison!' They've explained everything to me. Oh, they've not left me in the dark about anything. They are flattering your writers, but at the same time in Belgium, in Holland, in all the countries occupied by our troops, they've already put the bars up. No French book can go through any more except technical publications, manuals on Refraction or formulas for Cementation . . . But works of general culture, not one. None whatever!"[32]

His glance passed above my head, flitting about and coming up against the corners of the room like a lost night-bird. At last it seemed to find sanctuary in the darkest shelves – those where Racine, Ronsard, Rousseau[33] were aligned. His eyes stayed fixed there, and his voice went on with a groaning violence:

"Nothing, nothing, nobody!" And as if we hadn't yet understood or weighed the full measure of the threat: "Not only your modern writers! Not only your Péguy, your Proust, your Bergson . . .[34] But all the others! All those up there! The whole lot! Every one."

32. On the quota imposed on French books exported to German-occupied Europe, see the manifesto of the Editions de Minuit reprinted in Vercors, *Battle of Silence*, p. 174.

33. Pierre de Ronsard (ca. 1524–1584), poet; Jean-Jacques Rousseau (1712–1778), Swiss-French philosopher, political theorist, and writer.

34. Charles Péguy (1873–1914), poet and writer; Marcel Proust (1871–1922), novelist; Henri Bergson (1859–1941), philosopher.

His glance once more swept over the bindings which glittered softly in the twilight, with a kind of desperate caress. "They will put out the light altogether," he cried. "Never again will Europe be lit up by that flame." And his grave hollow voice made my breast echo with an unexpected and startling cry, a cry whose last syllable seemed drawn out into a wail.

"Nevermore!"

Once more the silence fell. Once more, but this time how much more tense and thick! Underneath our silences of the past I had indeed felt the submarine life of hidden emotions, conflicting and contradictory desires and thoughts swarming away like the warring creatures of the sea under the calm surface of the water. But beneath this silence, alas! there was nothing but a terrible sense of oppression. At last his voice broke the silence. It was gentle and distressed:

"I had a friend. He was like a brother. We had been to school together. We shared the same room at Stuttgart. We had spent three months together in Nuremberg. We never did anything without each other: I played my music to him; he read me his poems. He was sensitive and romantic. But he left me. He went to read his poems at Munich,[35] to some of his new friends. It was he who used always to be writing to me to come and join them. It was he that I saw in Paris with his friends. I have seen what they have made of him!"

He slowly shook his head as if he had to return a sorrowful refusal to some request.

"He was the most violent of them all. He mingled anger with mockery. One moment he would look at me with passion and cry: 'It's a poison! We've got to empty the creature of its poison!' The next moment he would give me little prods in the stomach with the end of his finger. 'They're scared stiff now, ha-ha! They're afraid of their pockets and for their stomach – for their trade and industry! That's all they think of! And as for the few others, we'll flatter them and put them to sleep, ha-ha! It will be easy!' He laughed at me till he went pink in the face. 'We'll buy their soul for a mess of pottage!'"

Werner paused for breath.

"I said to him: 'Have you grasped what you are doing? Have you

35. Capital of the southern German state of Bavaria and site of the founding of the Nazi party in 1919.

really *grasped* what it means?' He said, 'Do you think that is going to frighten us? Not with our kind of clearheadedness!' I said: 'Then you mean to seal up the tomb – and for ever?' He replied, 'It's a matter of life or death. Force is all you need to conquer with, but it's not enough to keep you masters. We know very well that an army counts for nothing in keeping you masters.' 'But at the price of the Spirit!' I cried. 'Not at that price!' 'The Spirit never dies,' he said. 'It has known it all before. It is born again from its ashes. We've got to build for a thousand years hence: first we must destroy.'[36] I looked at him. I looked right down into his pale eyes. He was quite sincere. That's the most terrible thing of all."

His eyes opened very wide, as if at the spectacle of some appalling murder: "They'll do what they say!" he cried, as if we wouldn't have believed him. "They'll do it systematically and doggedly. I know how those devils stop at nothing."

He shook his head like a dog with a bad ear. A murmur came from between his clenched teeth, the plaintive, passionate moan of the betrayed lover.

He hadn't moved. He was still standing rigidly and stiffly in the opening of the door, with his arms stretched out as if they had to carry hands of lead, and he was pale – not like wax, but like the plaster of certain decaying walls: grey, with whiter stains of saltpetre.

I saw him stoop slowly. He raised his hand and held it forward, palm down, towards my niece and myself, with the fingers a little bent. He clenched it and moved it up and down a little, while the expression on his face tightened with a kind of fierce energy. His lips parted, and I don't know what kind of appeal I thought he was going to make to us: I thought – yes, I thought that he was going to exhort us to rebel. But not a word crossed his lips. His mouth closed, and once again his eyes closed too. He stood up straight. His hands rose up the length of his body and, when they reached the level of his face, performed some unintelligible movements, something like certain figures in a Javanese religious dance. Then he seized his forehead and his temples, pressing down his eyelids with his stretched-out little fingers.

"They said to me: 'It's our right and our duty.' Our duty! . . . Happy is the man who discovers the path of his duty as easily as that."

36. The Nazis predicted their Third Reich would last for one thousand years; it was destroyed in a dozen.

He let his hands fall.

"At the crossroads you are told: 'Take that road there.'" He shook his head. "Well, that road doesn't lead up to the shining heights of the mountain-crest. One sees it going down to a gloomy valley and losing itself in the foul darkness of a dismal forest! . . . O God! Show me where *my* duty lies!"

He said – he almost shouted: "It is the Fight – it's the Great Battle of the Temporal with the Spiritual."

With pitiful insistency he fixed his eyes on the wooden angel carved above the window. The ecstatic, smiling angel, radiant with celestial calm.

Suddenly his expression seemed to relax, his body lost its stiffness, his face dropped a little towards the ground, he raised it.

"I stood on my rights," he said more naturally. "I applied to be reposted to a fighting unit, and at last they've granted me the favour. I am authorized to set off tomorrow."

I thought I saw the ghost of a smile on his lips when he amplified this with:

"Off to Hell."

He raised his arm towards the east – towards those vast plains where the wheat of the future will be fed on corpses.[37]

My niece's face gave me a shock: it was as pale as the moon. Her lips, like the rim of an opaline vase, were wide open, almost in the grimace of the Greek tragic masks, and, at the line where the hair rose from the forehead, I saw beads of sweat – not slowly gather, but gush out – yes, gush out.

I don't know if Werner von Ebrennac noticed. The pupils of his eyes and those of the girl seemed moored to each other, as a boat in a current is tied to a ring on the bank, and moored moreover by a line so tightly stretched that one would not have dared to pass a finger between the pairs of eyes. Ebrennac with one hand had taken hold of the door-handle; with his other he held the side of the doorway. Without moving his gaze a hair's-breadth, he slowly drew the door towards him. He said – in a voice that was strangely devoid of expression: "I wish you a very good night."

I thought that he was going to close the door and go; but not at all. He was looking at my niece. He looked at her, and said, or rather whispered, "Adieu."

He did not move; he remained quite motionless, and in his

37. Germany invaded the Soviet Union on 22 June 1941.

strained and motionless face his eyes were the most strained and motionless things of all, for they were bound to other eyes – too wide open, too pale – the eyes of my niece. That lasted and lasted – how long? – lasted right up to the moment when at length the girl moved her lips. Werner's eyes glittered. I heard:

"Adieu."

One could not have heard the word if one had not been waiting for it, but at last I did hear it. Von Ebrennac heard it too, and he drew himself up, and his face and his whole body seemed to relax as if they had taken a soothing bath.

He smiled, and in such a way that the last picture I had of him was a smiling one; then the door closed and his steps died away in the depths of the house.

The next day, when I came down to have my morning glass of milk, he was gone. My niece had got breakfast ready as she always did. She helped me to it in silence, and in silence we drank. Outside, a pale sun was shining through the mist. It struck me as being very cold.

October, 1941

Select Bibliography

The following list of books and articles is divided into two parts: the first section includes titles that particularly treat Vercors's writing and the Editions de Minuit, while the second comprises a sampling of works on the general subject of France during World War II.

I

Atack, Margaret. *Literature and the French Resistance: Cultural Politics and Narrative Forms, 1940–1950*. Manchester and New York: Manchester University Press, 1989. (A perceptive analysis of a wide selection of Resistance writing; see especially pp. 63–69.)

Bieber, Konrad F. *L'Allemagne vue par les écrivains de la Résistance française.* Geneva: Librairie E. Droz; and Lille: Librairie Giard, 1954. (Chap. 5, "Un ami exigeant de l'Allemagne: Vercors," traces Bruller's changing attitude toward Germany and the Germans before, during, and after the Second World War.)

Bliven, Naomi. "Keeping a Secret." *The New Yorker*, 8 November 1969, pp. 203–6. (A generally favorable review of Vercors's wartime memoir, *The Battle of Silence*.)

Brée, Germaine. *Twentieth-Century French Literature*. Chicago: The University of Chicago Press, translated 1983. (A sound introduction to the overall subject; see especially pp. 67–73.)

Brée, Germaine, and Bernauer, George, eds. *Defeat and Beyond: An Anthology of French Wartime Writing, 1940–1945*. New York: Pantheon Books, 1970. (This useful collection includes a translation of Pierre Lescure's manifesto for the Editions de Minuit on pp. 247–48.)

Brodin, Pierre. *Présences contemporaines. Vol. 1, Littérature*. Paris: Nouvelles Editions Debresse, 1956. (Pp. 321 and 323–31 include a list of Vercors's publications and an analysis of some of them together with biographical information.)

Caute, David. *The Fellow-Travellers: A Postscript to the Enlightenment*. London: Weidenfeld and Nicolson, 1973. (Contains random references to Vercors's various political activities after the Second World War.)

Debû-Bridel, Jacques. *Les Editions de Minuit: Historique et bibliographie.*

Select Bibliography

Paris: Aux Editions de Minuit, 1945. (A brief, "official" history of the publishing enterprise by one of its leading figures.)

———, ed. *La Résistance intellectuelle: Textes et témoignages*. Paris: Julliard, 1970. (A collection of statements by Resistance members, some associated with Editions de Minuit including the editor.)

Fouché, Pascal. *L'Edition française sous l'Occupation, 1940–1944*. 2 vols. Paris: Bibliothèque de la littérature française contemporaine de l'Université Paris 7, 1987. (The most comprehensive account of the French publishing industry during the German Occupation.)

John, S. Beynon. "The Ambiguous Invader: Images of the German in Some French Fiction about the Occupation of 1940–44." *Journal of European Studies* 16 (1986): 187–200. (Concludes that Vercors's story "was already anachronistic by the time it appeared.")

King, J.H. "Language and Silence: Some Aspects of French Writing and the French Resistance." *European Studies Review* 3 (1972): 227–38. (Thoughtful treatment of Resistance literature in relation to the linguistic concept of silence.)

Koestler, Arthur. *The Yogi and the Commissar and other Essays*. London: Jonathan Cape, 1945. (Includes the 1943 article "The French 'Flu'" highly critical of the "exasperating" novel by Vercors.)

Kolbert, Jack. "Vercors: Bibliography." In *A Critical Bibliography of French Literature: The 20th Century* edited by Richard A. Brooks. Syracuse, N.Y.: Syracuse University Press, 1980. (A short, annotated list of biographical and general studies of Vercors, including references to reviews of several of his books.)

Konstantinovič, Radivoje D. *Vercors écrivain et dessinateur*. Paris: Klincksieck, 1969. (The most thorough biographical and literary study of Vercors as artist and writer.)

Liebling, A.J., ed. *The Republic of Silence*. New York: Harcourt Brace, 1947. (Pp. 171–75 of this anthology include a discussion of the novel and the publishing firm.)

Lottman, Herbert R. *The Left Bank: Writers, Artists, and Politics from the Popular Front to the Cold War*. Boston: Houghton Mifflin, 1982. (Chap. 21, "Midnight Presses," presents a positive account of the accomplishments of Editions de Minuit and of Vercors.)

Metzger, L., ed. *Contemporary Authors* Vol. 12. Detroit: Gale Research, 1984. (The entry for Jean Bruller contains a complete listing of his publications.)

Paulhan, Jean, and Aury, Dominique. *La Patrie se fait tous les jours: Textes français, 1939–1945*. Paris: Les Editions de Minuit, 1947. (This extensive anthology includes numerous extracts from works published by Editions de Minuit.)

Sartre, Jean-Paul. *What is Literature?* London: Methuen, translated 1950.

(The brief discussion of Vercors's novel predicted that it would "no longer excite anyone" a half century after its publication.)

Seghers, Pierre. *La Résistance et ses poètes (France 1940/1945).* 3d rev. ed. Paris: Editions Seghers, 1974. (Briefly discusses poetry published by Editions de Minuit and reprints two poems by Vercors.)

Travaux et Recherches sur la guerre: Bilan d'un séminaire, 1981–1984, Bulletin de l'institut d'histoire du temps présent, supplement no. 7 (1985), Série "Seconde guerre mondiale," no. 1. [Paris], 1985. (Pp. 24–26 contain a biographical sketch of Vercors.)

Vercors. *The Battle of Silence.* New York: Holt, Rinehart, and Winston, translated 1968. (The author's indispensable war memoirs.)

———. *Guiding Star.* New York: Macmillan, translated 1946. (The second clandestine novel published by the author also treats life under the Occupation.)

———. *Portrait d'une amitié et d'autres morts mémorables.* Paris: Editions Albin Michel, 1954. (Includes a discussion of Vercors's attitude toward war before 1939 and his tributes to Resistance figures killed by the Germans.)

II

Azéma, Jean-Pierre. *From Munich to the Liberation, 1938–1944.* Cambridge University Press, translated 1984. (This sixth volume in *The Cambridge History of Modern France* provides perhaps the most satisfactory general treatment of the period it covers.)

Bloch, Marc. *Strange Defeat: A Statement of Evidence Written in 1940.* London: Oxford University Press, translated 1949. (The classic account by a great French historian.)

Cairns, John C. "Along the Road Back to France, 1940." *American Historical Review* 64 (1959): 583–603. (An excellent historiographical article.)

Chapman, Guy. *Why France Collapsed.* London: Cassell, 1968. (A reasoned analysis of this highly controversial question.)

Chatwin, Bruce. "An Aesthete at War." *The New York Review of Books,* 5 March 1981, pp. 21–25. (Review essay on Ernst Jünger and his diaries from wartime France.)

Cobb, Richard. *French and Germans, Germans and French: A Personal Interpretation of France under Two Occupations, 1914–1918/1940–1944.* Hanover, New Hampshire: University Press of New England for Brandeis University Press, 1983. (The insightful observations of an acknowledged expert on French life in its historical context.)

Dank, Milton. *The French against the French: Collaboration and Resistance.* Philadelphia: J.B. Lippincott, 1974. (A sound introductory treatment.)

Gordon, Bertram M. *Collaborationism in France during the Second World War.*

Ithaca, New York: Cornell University Press, 1980. (This is a superior treatment of a complicated subject.)

Hoffmann, Stanley. *Decline or Renewal? France since the 1930s*, New York: Viking Press, 1974. (A collection of essays on important topics by a specialist on contemporary France.)

Johnson, Douglas. *France*. London: Thames and Hudson, 1969. (A fine, shorter history.)

Jünger, Ernst. *Werke*. Vol. 2. Stuttgart: Ernst Klett Verlag, 1960. (Includes his diary of the 1940 French campaign, *Gärten und Straßen*.)

Kedward, H.R. *Occupied France: Collaboration and Resistance*. Oxford and New York: Basil Blackwell, 1985. (A superb overview of France's wartime experience.)

——. *Resistance in Vichy France: A Study of Ideas and Motivation in the Southern Zone, 1940–1942*. Oxford and New York: Oxford University Press, 1978. (One of the best introductions to the subject of the French Resistance.)

Marrus, Michael R., and Paxton, Robert O. *Vichy France and the Jews*. New York: Basic Books, 1981. (The standard work on the topic that exposes the role of the Vichy government in accelerating the murder of Jews from France by the Nazis.)

Michel, Henri. *Bibliographie critique de la Résistance*. Paris: Institut Pédagogique National, 1964. (A helpful compilation of titles.)

——. *Vichy Année 40*. Paris: Robert Laffont, 1966. (Detailed treatment of the establishment of the Vichy regime.)

Milward, Alan S. *The New Order and the French Economy*. Oxford: Clarendon Press, 1970. (The most reliable analysis of the economic impact of the German Occupation on France.)

Noguères, Henri et al. *Histoire de la Résistance en France de 1940 à 1945*. Vol. 1, *La première année, Juin 1940–Juin 1941*. Vol. 2, *L'Armée de l'ombre, Juillet 1941–Octobre 1942*. Paris: Robert Laffont, 1967 and 1969. (The first volumes in a massive study of the French Resistance.)

Novick, Peter. *The Resistance versus Vichy: The Purge of Collaborators in Liberated France*. London: Chatto and Windus, 1968. (A careful assessment based on the evidence.)

Paxton, Robert O. *Vichy France: Old Guard and New Order, 1940–1944*. New York: Knopf, 1972. (Perhaps the best one-volume history of the Vichy regime.)

Pryce-Jones, David. *Paris in the Third Reich: A History of the German Occupation, 1940–1944*. New York: Holt, Rinehart, and Winston, 1981. (Valuable especially for its photographs.)

Sadoun, Marc. *Les Socialistes sous l'Occupation: Résistance et collaboration*. Paris: Presses de la Fondation Nationale des Sciences Politiques, 1982.

(Standard account of the activities of the French Socialist party during the war.)

Soucy, Robert. *Fascist Intellectual: Drieu la Rochelle.* Berkeley and Los Angeles: University of California Press, 1979. (Biography of the leading collaborationist editor and writer.)

Sweets, John F. *Choices in Vichy France: The French under Nazi Occupation.* New York: Oxford University Press, 1986. (Revealing case study of Occupation and Resistance in Clermont-Ferrand.)

——. *The Politics of Resistance in France, 1940–1944: A History of the Mouvements unis de la Résistance.* Dekalb, Illinois: Northern Illinois University Press, 1976. (An excellent monograph on a leading Resistance organization.)

Warner, Geoffrey. *Pierre Laval and the Eclipse of France.* London: Eyre and Spottiswoode, 1968. (The most satisfying biography of any Vichy leader.)

Werth, Alexander. *France, 1940–1955.* New York: Henry Holt, 1956. (A factual account by a knowledgeable foreign correspondent.)

Wilkinson, James D. *The Intellectual Resistance in Europe.* Cambridge, Mass.: Harvard University Press, 1981. (A superb study, one-third of which is devoted to the experience of French intellectuals during and immediately following the war.)